THE
STRANGER
GAME

CYLIN BUSBY

THE
STRANGER
GAME

BALZER + BRAY

An Imprint of HarperCollins*Publishers*

Balzer + Bray is an imprint of HarperCollins Publishers.

The Stranger Game

Copyright © 2016 by Cylin Busby

All rights reserved. Printed in the United States of America. No part
of this book may be used or reproduced in any manner whatsoever
without written permission except in the case of brief quotations
embodied in critical articles and reviews. For information address
HarperCollins Children's Books, a division of HarperCollins
Publishers, 195 Broadway, New York, NY 10007.

www.epicreads.com

Library of Congress Control Number: 2016930985
ISBN 978-0-06-235460-0

Typography by Sarah Creech

16 17 18 19 20   PC/RRDH   10 9 8 7 6 5 4 3 2 1

First Edition

For Nanci, my partner in crime

PROLOGUE

I KNEW MY SISTER was dead. I felt it in my body, as if my bones could tell me the truth. They were, after all, her bones too. The same parents had created us, we carried the same DNA, the stuff that makes us who we are. I even looked like her: a little twin, a few years younger. And both of us were images of Mom, or how she was in her high school yearbook, with long blond hair and hazel eyes.

When I looked in the mirror, I didn't just see my own face but my sister's too, the one from the Missing posters we had put up all over Mapleview four years ago—the one on the news, in newspapers across the country. Now that my braces were off I could even smile like her, the way she had in our last family photo. The smile of a girl who was head cheerleader. Who had an older boyfriend. Who had secrets.

I wanted so much to believe she was alive, to cling to hope like

Mom. I tried. I let myself imagine that Sarah might walk through the door any day. At night, that hope failed me. In my nightmares I saw all the terrible things that happen to girls like Sarah. When I woke, the vivid images still in my mind, my heart racing, I would lie in bed and watch the lights from the occasional car move over my ceiling and walls and think about the people in those cars. Where were they going? Where had they been, out so late? What were their lives like, lives without the giant gaping hole that is left when someone in your family goes missing?

I tried to picture Sarah now, how she might look: older, her hair longer or shorter, her skin tanned golden like it had been the last time I saw her. As the days ticked by, the volume of her absence increased. Weeks turned into months and then into years. I knew the truth, even if I could never speak of it to anyone. I knew the darkened bedroom next to mine would always be empty, the door always shut, because this time Sarah wasn't coming back.

CHAPTER 1

THE PHONE NEVER REALLY rang at the help line. Instead, a red light lit up on the keypad, and then the incoming number slowly scrolled onto the screen with the approximate location of the caller. All you had to do was push the button next to the red light to accept the call and speak into the headset: "Teen Help Line. Hi, this is Nico, what's your name?"

We had a script we were supposed to follow, and hours of training before we were allowed to answer incoming calls. Even then, Marcia, the supervisor, paced the room, watching over us and clicking on to calls with her own master headset. She would come and stand behind you and write notes if she had something she thought you should say. If a call got totally out of control, she was there to switch lines and take over.

When I showed up to volunteer, usually one afternoon a week, there was always a volunteer older than me, with more experience.

They would take most of the calls and I would just sit and listen. "No better training than this, watching what the other volunteers do, how they react," Marcia said, probably thinking that I was bummed I didn't get to take more calls. That wasn't the case, though—far from it. I was actually relieved. For months, I had been terrified I would take a call and say or do the wrong thing. We had people's lives in our hands here; so many of them called in ready to do something serious: hurting themselves or someone else. I was happy to sit and listen in, with no responsibility of my own. But sometimes, like tonight, Marcia would ask me to take a call.

"That's you, Nico, line two," she said. The two other volunteers, Amber and Kerri, were already on calls, and for some reason, our fourth person hadn't shown up.

I put down the slice of pizza I was eating and wiped my hands quickly before pressing the button next to the red light. "Teen Help Line." I barely got the words out before I heard her on the other side. Crying.

"Oh, there's really someone there?" A small voice sniffled. "A real person?"

"My name is Nico, what's yours?" I followed the script, Marcia nodding as I spoke. The caller's name and number came up on the screen. She was on a cell phone outside Denver. She wasn't lying about her name, like lots of callers did; the phone was registered to her. I listened closely as she talked, about the girls at her school and how they were treating her, about how she had started cutting and wanted to stop but didn't know how. "Sometimes I think about just running away, like, just starting over somewhere. You know? Just disappearing," the girl said.

A shiver ran down my spine. "I know, I totally understand. We all feel that way sometimes. . . ." I gave the advice I was supposed to, clicked the resource link next to her location, and gave her the names and numbers of the places closest to her where she could get help. But the whole time, my mind was not really on this crying girl. I was thinking of Sarah. Would I know her if she called? That couldn't happen—would never happen. Coincidences like that were for the movies, not real life. Still, part of me had to admit the truth about why I had chosen to volunteer at the help line to meet the school community service requirement.

I could have been at the animal hospital, nursing a baby rabbit back to health.

Or at Mapleview Home for Seniors, reading to some nice old blind lady.

But here I was, answering calls from teens who wanted to disappear—and then sometimes did.

By the time I ended the call, the Denver girl had stopped crying. Marcia looked over and gave me a smile and a thumbs-up, even though I could tell she was already listening to another call. I noticed with a start that it was 9:02. I dug my community service form out of my backpack and put it on her desk on my way out.

"Nico," Marcia called to me as I was almost at the elevators. "Great work tonight, really," she said. Her eyes were on the form I'd left on her desk. "Where am I supposed to sign this?"

I walked back to her desk and showed her. "But you also have to fill out the evaluation section," I reminded her. "So I'll pick it up from you later."

"Give me a minute and I'll do it right now."

I glanced at the backlit clock on the wall. Now it was 9:05. "I can't, I have to go," I said.

"Really, it'll just take a sec," she insisted.

I stood next to her desk for a moment while she wrote something on the lines. Her black pen moved so slowly. Halfway done. 9:07. I could feel my heart thumping in my chest.

"I'll get it from you next week," I said, running out the door. I didn't give her a chance to answer. I pressed the elevator button hard, over and over, until the doors opened. I did the math in my head. By the time I got to the lobby and out the doors, it would be 9:10. I felt my phone vibrating in my bag before I even made it outside.

There was Mom, her car idling by the curb where she always parked. I could see the bluish light of her cell phone reflected on her face, the lines on her forehead deep and worried. I moved fast over the sidewalk and across the grass, where bits of slushy spring snow soaked my sneakers. I tapped the passenger side window. She looked up at me and for a moment I could see the shock on her face. In the dark, with my long blond hair down under my hood, she thought I was someone else. I knew who.

I pushed the hood back, showing her my face. She smiled and rolled the window down.

"You scared me! Come on, get in, it's freezing."

I got into the warm car, smelling leather and Mom's perfume.

"You're late, and I tried to call you. Nico—"

"Not my fault. You know we aren't allowed to even take our phones out in the center. And Marcia was filling out my school forms and taking her time."

Mom didn't say anything, just looked into the mirror as she pulled out of the spot. She didn't have to say anything. I knew how she worried, how unacceptable it was to make her feel like that. Our agreement about always being in touch, no matter what. But sometimes, it was impossible. Impossible to be perfect, to always be on time, to never, ever make Mom and Dad worry about me the way they had about her.

"What's the homework situation?" Mom finally spoke in a normal tone of voice as she turned left onto the street that led to our neighborhood.

"Almost done. I have a chapter to read for chemistry."

"And you ate already?" she asked.

"I ate, Mom," I answered with a sigh. Always the same questions. Always the same answers.

She pulled into our driveway, brightly lit by two floodlights over the double garage doors and lanterns on either side of the front door. As we waited for a garage door to open, Mom turned to me. "You know that I'm so proud of you for working at the help line, don't you? Your dad is too. I want you to know that."

I nodded, giving her a weak smile. What wasn't said, the dark undercurrent of her compliment: *You're not like her.* I was that age now, the age she was when the trouble really started. When she ran away the first time. But I was so different, a good girl. Straight-A student. Volunteer. Captain of the tennis team. Mom and Dad didn't have to worry about me. I wasn't like Sarah and I never would be.

In Mom's headlights, I could see the three bikes lined up in the garage: mine, Mom's, and Dad's. The police had found Sarah's bike at the park the day she went missing, and they never gave it back to us. I pictured it in some dark evidence-storage room, a paper tag with Sarah's name on it dangling from the silver handlebars. Black powder covering the places they had dusted it for fingerprints, the tires now flat and cracked with age, the purple paint peeling and rusted. No one would ride that bike ever again.

SARAH

THE FIRST NIGHT WASN'T that bad. The room was dark, and I was used to sleeping with the lights on. But I didn't want to make them mad, so I didn't say anything, I didn't complain, I didn't cry.

I could hear them in the next room talking, the clink of ice in a glass. Much later, the voices got louder, and one said, "A girl! We got a real girl!"

More voices, so loud I couldn't sleep. Then someone opened the door, unlocked it from outside, and a shaft of light came in, falling on my face. I closed my eyes fast and pretended to be asleep. I had to breathe so slowly, so carefully. They didn't come into the room, just stood in the doorway and looked at me, whispering. "There she is, I told you!"

"I can't believe it, and she's beautiful," another voice said.

"Like an angel."

"Let's hope she acts like one." Someone laughed.

The door closed and I heard the lock slide into place. I was alone again, in the dark.

CHAPTER 2

RIGHT AFTER SARAH WENT missing, people everywhere thought they saw her. In the shampoo aisle of a Target in Missouri. Sitting in a parked car at a gas station just outside Las Vegas. At a fall pumpkin festival in Ohio. Walking with an older woman at a Best Buy in Florida.

They called the number printed on the Missing poster and gave all the information. She was the right height, had long blond hair (or, in one case, her hair had been cut short and dyed black, to disguise her—but the person was still sure it was Sarah). She was wearing jeans and a dusty pink tank top, just like in the photo. Sometimes she was wearing sunglasses or a hat. Or the tank was white, not pink. Or her shirt had changed. And her jeans. Maybe it was a dress or shorts. Maybe it was the outfit she was wearing that day: a white sleeveless dress that came to the knee, a thin gray cardigan, and brown suede boots. But everyone was sure they had found Sarah—the beautiful, blond fifteen-year-old girl who had disappeared. Who had gone to meet her boyfriend at the park and never come home.

The police and later the Center for Missing Children followed up on every lead. They had officers question people at stores, review surveillance tapes, interview local convicts—and, perhaps worst of all, interrogate convicted rapists and child molesters—in every town where someone thought they had seen Sarah.

The first time we got a call, just four days after Sarah disappeared, my parents were sure they had found her. As if it would be that easy. Mom jumped every time the phone rang. And on that afternoon, she could see on caller ID that it was the police station. She took a deep breath, swallowed, ran her palms down the front of her pants, then picked up the phone.

It was a sighting at a Target store in Missouri, where Sarah had been reportedly browsing in the shampoo aisle. My sister was vain about her blond hair and wouldn't use anything but a salon shampoo. It just didn't make sense. But there she was, shopping for shampoo and wearing, it seemed, an identical outfit to what she had on in the Missing poster.

The detectives told Mom and Dad they would call again in an hour with more information. The moment Mom put the phone down, she turned to me. "It's her, they found her. Thank God."

She sat down beside me on the couch and we stayed like that for the whole hour, waiting for them to call again, while Dad paced in the kitchen. I had this weird feeling that if I moved, if I stood up and went to the bathroom or into the kitchen for a drink, somehow the spell would be broken and Sarah would vanish again. When the phone finally rang, Dad snatched it, his face growing ashen as he listened, nodding and saying "uh-huh" every few seconds.

"What is it? What is he saying? Is she okay?" Mom whispered. Dad only shook his head. Mom covered her mouth and quietly sobbed.

"It's not her," Dad said, then took the phone into the kitchen to talk about next steps in the investigation. And with those three little words their hopes were crushed. Mom followed him, asking things like "Are they sure?" and "How do they know?" I stayed on the couch in the living room alone for what felt like hours, listening to Mom weep. No one reminded me to brush my teeth. No one told me to go to bed. Finally I went upstairs on my own, down the dark hallway, past Sarah's bedroom. I reached in and pulled her door shut before I went into my own room.

The calls came almost every day after that—from all over, fast and furious. And with each false alarm, I watched Mom turn in on herself, her hair sprouting white-gray roots among the honey blond, tiny lines appearing around her eyes and lips as her weight plummeted. She had always been a thin woman, but now, even without her twice-weekly Pilates classes, she grew bony and fragile. Dad became sullen and quiet, finally returning to work two weeks after Sarah disappeared, and then quickly throwing himself into a new merger. His hours got longer: he left at dawn and came home long after we had eaten dinner. It was as if he couldn't bear to be around us, the blond girls, the constant reminder that his favorite was gone. Mom would practically attack him from the moment he arrived home, weary and stooped, carrying his briefcase like a heavy weight, and tell him all the updates about the search for Sarah in a quick rush, following him into the den, where he would pour himself a Scotch.

Mom never went back to her part-time job at the law firm, instead taking on the full-time job of running the search for Sarah. The home office turned into a command post, with a huge poster of the United States taped to one wall, red pushpins at every location where someone thought they had seen Sarah. By the end of the first month, it looked like most of the United States had chicken pox.

I went back to school, even though I had missed the first couple of weeks of seventh grade. Every morning, I would wake, barely rested, a gritty feeling under my eyelids, and just for a moment forget that Sarah was gone. Sometimes I wouldn't remember until I'd stumbled to the bathroom or heard Mom telling me it was time for school. Then it would come back to me all in a rush, that sick feeling of dread, of emptiness. It wasn't a bad dream. It wasn't a book I had read, a movie we had watched. It was real.

At first, school was no escape. I was known as "Sarah's little sister" or "*that* girl." People always asked—they had to ask: Was there any news? How are your parents? But after a couple of weeks the worried looks from teachers and visits to the counselor's office were less frequent. Sarah had gone missing in August, and as we tumbled into October and then November, the holidays loomed like the mouth of a dark cave that no one wanted to enter. I had been walking around in a daze, taking the pills that Mom's doctor gave her, not really connecting with anyone at school. I hadn't noticed the new girl who started at our school that fall. A girl who had never known Sarah, who didn't know anything about me. Except one thing.

"You lost a lot of weight, huh?" she said, joining me at my locker after English class one day. I hadn't been trying to, but she was right. A growth spurt and lack of appetite over the past few months had led me to thin out. I thought no one had noticed.

"Me too, or I'm trying to," she whispered, leaning in close as she walked with me to my next class. "I wanted to make a new start at this school, and I didn't want to be known as the fat girl, you know, so I went on a cleanse. . . ." She smiled and I noticed that just the ends of her dark curls were dyed a light purple hue. "You're Nico, right? I love your name. I'm Tessa." The bell rang and cut her off. "Well, see you at lunch."

Because of our last names, Morris and Montford, Tessa was seated near me in almost every class. She also played tennis—not well, but it was enough to join the team. And while Mom still insisted on driving me to school every day and walking me through the gates, watching until I was inside the building, she slowly came around to the idea of letting Tessa's mom drive us home after tennis practice some days. It was so freeing to be in someone else's car for a change, to go out for fro-yo and talk about boys and school—anything but my missing sister.

With Tessa it was easy to forget—and I did—until there would be a Sarah sighting, and then it would all come crashing down, especially if my parents took the report seriously enough to pull me out of school. The first time it happened was only about six months after Sarah went missing.

I knew something was wrong when I heard the announcement over the loudspeaker that I should report to the office and collect my things, as I would be leaving for the day. I knew at once it had to do with Sarah—and so did everyone else. Their eyes were on me as I stuffed my notebooks into my backpack and made my way from the classroom. I heard whispers, or imagined I did. Tessa bravely stood up and told our English teacher that she would be walking me to the office. I liked how she didn't ask.

We walked the hallway in silence, the sound of footsteps echoing. Without a word, Tessa took my hand in hers and squeezed hard.

In the school office, Mom waited for me, pale and red-eyed. "They think they've found her," she started to say, but that was nothing new. When I pulled a face, she added, "It's a body." She broke down, sobbing. I didn't know what to do so I patted her shoulder, knowing that everyone who worked in the school office was watching us. I wanted to say *It won't be her, Mom*, but I couldn't form the words.

I walked behind her to the car, where Dad waited for us. I slipped into the backseat and pulled on my seat belt almost robotically. A *body*. I felt my stomach roll over at the word.

"We should have left her at school," Dad said, as if I wasn't there.

"I want her with us." Mom turned to him. "Where is she supposed to go after, if . . ."

"She could have gone home with someone. That girl with the purple hair, whoever. Christ," Dad mumbled, pulling out of the parking lot.

Mom said nothing for a moment, then she turned and her eyes locked on mine. There was no way she was letting me out of her sight for any longer than she had to. "We'll have a police escort," she explained to me calmly, "or it would take two hours to get there."

We sped along the highway, doing close to ninety miles an hour, a police cruiser with lights swirling leading the way. Mom was calm enough to fill me in on the basics: the body was that of a young blond woman, too decomposed for easy identification. They needed us to come and have a look, to see if we recognized the clothing, the shoes . . . what was left. No one spoke for the rest of the drive, although Mom continued to cry quietly on and off.

My memories of that afternoon are so vivid: the sound of gravel under the car tires as we pulled off the paved road, the clearing in the trees, water glittering dark and blue in the distance, a rusted chain drawn across the end of the path, a No Trespassing sign. A man in a dark suit, glasses pushed up on his head, his hands covered in surgical gloves, walking toward the car as we pulled in. Mom opening the door before we had stopped, dust from the gravel on her black boots. The man holding up his hands, then the words: "It's not her."

It's not her.

This time, our hopes were not dashed—they were raised. We were elated. Mom collapsed to the ground, sobbing as the man explained quietly how sure they were. How it couldn't be her. The girl had a scar where her appendix had been removed. Dad crouched next to Mom, his arms around her, his face unreadable.

"I knew it wasn't her, I knew it. She's still alive, I know it, I know it, I can feel it, I'm her mother. . . ." Mom couldn't stop talking. The man in the gloves just nodded and the other cops stood around uncomfortably.

I climbed from the car and looked out over the dusty quarry to where a body was covered with a white sheet. Other cops and detectives were poking around the tall grass with long poles, putting evidence into plastic bags.

That wasn't my sister under that sheet. But it was still someone. Some blond girl, who had once been living and now was dead. Someone's daughter. Someone's sister.

CHAPTER 3

I WISH THAT I could say that was the last time my parents had to look at a body, but it wasn't. After that first time at the quarry, there were others: in the morgue of a town a half hour away; in photos shown by detectives; and once more, a year after Sarah disappeared, at a location far from our home—and that was body parts, found stuffed in a suitcase and left in a dump up north. Thankfully they didn't take me along for that excruciating ride, for that horrifying misidentification. I was thirteen, old enough to be left at home. Of course, I wasn't left alone. My parents would never do that. They had a detective sit in a cruiser outside the house while they went to look at the hands and clothing of the dead girl in the suitcase. So many dead girls, so many blond girls—but none of them were Sarah.

About two years after Sarah disappeared, there were no more bodies, no more calls. Mom was pretty desperate, phoning the detectives every week, asking for new information or leads. She was always met with the same reply: there was nothing. I knew she had reached a new level of desperation when I came home one day after tennis practice to find someone named Madame Azul sitting at our kitchen table—frizzy gray hair, several mismatched cheap necklaces of wooden beads strung around her wrinkled neck, a flowing purple printed polyester dress. I knew at first sight what she was—I had seen women like her at the carnival every summer: get your palm read, know your future, only five dollars. Women like this would usually be sitting at a folding table, swathed in polyester scarves, a cheap crystal ball propped in front of them.

Once, when we were younger, I remember Sarah having her palm read by a mystic at the summer fair. "See this line here," the woman said, pointing to a crease in her palm. "You will have a long and happy life. This line says your husband will be handsome. Oh! I think you're going to be blessed with twins—little girls!"

Sarah had grinned at Mom and Dad, and then it was my turn. But I clenched my fist tight and shook my head. I didn't want to know what the lines on my hand had to tell me.

"Nico, this is Azul. She's here to talk to us about Sarah." Mom pulled out a chair, motioning for me to sit down.

I stood next to the table, my tennis bag still slung over one shoulder. "Azul?" I said like it was a question. I saw Mom's face tighten.

"After I had my Reiki training, I adopted a new name for myself," the old lady said. She turned to Mom and added quietly, "My given name was weighed down with past lives and karma that I needed to release. You understand."

Mom nodded as if this made total sense. "Nico, please, join us. Azul had a dream about Sarah and she just wanted to come by and tell us about it." I dropped my tennis bag on the floor and took a seat.

Azul went on to tell Mom that she had seen Sarah's face on the news and on the posters around town years ago—of course, everyone had. But more recently, she had a dream—a vision, really—of my sister. I almost spoke up then—there had been a newspaper article a week ago revisiting the case. The headline had read: Where Is Sarah Morris? The reporter had spoken to my parents and interviewed both Max and Paula, Sarah's boyfriend and best friend. The article was full of loose ends, leads to nowhere. And, to be honest, it made Paula and Max look somewhat awful, featuring a photo of them sitting together, a big smile on Paula's face. I wondered if Azul's "dream" might have been inspired not by divine intervention but by the Sunday paper.

"I see water." Azul started to speak, with her eyes closed. "It's a happy vision, peaceful." She opened her eyes. "Did you ever go on a vacation to a lake or near a stream or river?"

Mom shook her head. "Not that I can think of. Could there be snow? The mountains?"

I knew Mom was thinking of Max's family cabin. It was near a lake. "This is a wooded area, very peaceful. . . ." Azul closed her eyes again and reached for Mom's hand. "That's all I'm getting for now, but if I meditate on it, I know I'll see more."

Mom let out a sigh with a small smile—a body of water in a wooded area didn't give us any new information. Everyone knew that Sarah had disappeared at MacArthur Park, where there were woods and a reservoir. Of course Azul would "see" that.

"So, how much does this cost—your meditation, your vision?" I asked bluntly.

Azul shook her head. "I just wanted to share it with you," she said, standing. "If the information is helpful, then blessed be." The metal bracelets on her wrists clanged together as she leaned in to embrace Mom. "Here's my card if you ever want to talk."

I knew that Mom would want to talk. And she did. Not long after Azul's unscheduled visit, Mom made an actual appointment with her and made sure Dad was home too. I could tell he believed in Azul about as much as I did, but what could we do? The detectives had come up with nothing. In fact, they hadn't even called in months. Even after the big article, there were no new leads, just renewed speculation about Paula and Max. Everyone else seemed to have forgotten about Sarah, except for us . . . and Azul.

She came by one evening after dinner, and Mom cleared the dining room table and dimmed the lights, laughing at herself. "I don't really know how to host a séance!" she joked. I didn't point out that a séance was used to contact the dead. Is that what we were doing?

Azul showed up smelling strongly of pine incense. As she moved through our house, touching various objects and photos, her purple caftan wafted behind her, leaving a scent of stale Christmas trees. Once we were all seated at the table, Azul asked that we hold hands. I reached awkwardly across the table to take Dad's hand, embarrassed that my palms were sweating. I tried to remember the last time my hand had been in his—years ago, maybe crossing a street?

Azul said some sort of incantation and bowed her head, so we all did the same. "I'll need something of Sarah's, something she wore or kept close to her," Azul said, raising her head. Mom glanced over at me, thinking.

"I can get something," I said, and pushed back my chair to go upstairs. I turned the knob of Sarah's door slowly, reaching in to flip the switch while my feet were still firmly in the hallway. Something about having a psychic downstairs had me spooked—like I would look into the mirror and see Sarah looking back at me, her hair dripping with seaweed. But her room was the same, quiet and pink, unchanged. I looked around and grabbed the first thing I saw—a little white teddy bear that sat on her bed. The bear was wearing a black beret and had been a gift from when Gram went to Paris years ago. I had one too, but my bear's beret was yellow.

I went downstairs, handing the bear to Azul as if it were made of glass. She turned it over in her hands, her clunky rings banging against the wooden table. Finally, she held it to her chest, her brace-lets clanging down her arm, and started humming. Dad caught my eye, raising his brows. Mom was looking only at Azul, her eyes huge.

"I have a message," Azul said, putting the white bear down on the table. I looked at it, with its stupid beret. What were we doing?

"Your daughter has left this plane of existence," Azul went on. I felt a rushing sound in my ears as Mom let out a gasp and swallowed back a sob. Dad moved closer to her, putting an arm around her back.

"What do you mean?" Mom asked. "You said you saw her by a lake, some peaceful vision."

Azul nodded, reaching over to take Mom's hand. "Yes, she is at peace. I still see trees, so many trees, and water. . . ."

Mom pulled her hand back from Azul. "Where is she?" she demanded.

"It's a place she knows, she's been there many times before. She loves this place, it's peaceful to her." Azul spoke with her eyes closed.

"The park—the reservoir?" Dad finally asked. He hadn't been there for Azul's first visit, where I figured out her scam. But he looked like he was starting to get it now.

"Is it the park?" Mom asked. I felt a cold sweat racing over my scalp with a thousand prickles.

"I'm not sure where it is," Azul answered. "But . . . someone knows, someone close to her. There is someone who isn't telling you everything."

Oh really, I thought. But looking at Mom, I could see her leaning in, holding on to Azul's hand now. "Who knows?" she asked.

Azul's eyes opened and she looked around the table. "It's someone you would never expect." She rubbed her hands together and her bracelets clanged in an annoyingly loud way in the quiet room.

"Is that all?" Dad asked. I could tell from his tone he was over this whole thing.

Azul sighed dramatically and closed her eyes. She started humming again. Then suddenly, she stopped. I could hear myself breathing, waiting for what she might say. "That's all my spirits are showing me right now," she said, shaking her head.

. . .

Later, after she was gone, I heard Mom and Dad in the kitchen, arguing. Well, mostly Dad arguing. "So we had to pay two hundred and fifty dollars for her to tell us nothing—because that's what her 'spirits' had for us?" he yelled. Mom was talking more quietly, and I tried to hear, but whatever she said to him calmed him down. Still, when they came up to bed I heard him say, "For another five hundred, maybe she can tell us what Sarah was wearing in those photos on the Missing poster!"

Mom knocked quietly on my door and came into my room, knowing that I would still be up. "Kind of lame, huh?" I smiled, trying to make light of the visit from Azul. She sat down on my bed, moving over the notebooks near my feet.

"I don't know what to believe anymore." She sighed. "I thought she might really have had a vision, or something." She looked down at my bedspread, picking off a piece of lint. "I'm sorry to put you and your father through that."

I shrugged. "You had to try, right?" I asked. I hoped that she would just forget about the whole thing and say good night, but instead she glanced up at me, looking hard into my eyes.

"What do you think she meant—that someone knows something they aren't saying?"

I felt my throat tighten, but I managed a casual shrug. "What I'd like to know is what her real name was, before she changed it to a color." I tried for a light laugh, opening my history book.

She smiled. "Oh, is that what Azul means? Blue, right? I guess I didn't put that together." I saw her shoulders slump and she shook her head, as if trying to forget the whole night. She stood up and walked to my dresser, picking up Sarah's bear that I had left there.

"I was going to put it back," I started to say, hearing my voice take on a defensive tone. And I had meant to. I just didn't want to go into Sarah's room, in the dark—not after what Azul had said.

"That's okay, I'll do it," Mom said, holding the white bear delicately. She pulled it into her chest and hugged it tightly. "Good night, sweetie. Don't stay up too late, okay?"

With all the false alarms my parents had to weather, all the bodies they had to identify, and the so-called psychic visions, Mom was decidedly unenthusiastic when the call came in that afternoon. It was almost four years after Sarah's disappearance and two years after our visits from Azul, and every day had brought nothing but more disappointments.

The phone rang in Mom's office, a special line specifically set up for tips about Sarah or for Mom's assistance in other cases of missing kids. I wouldn't even have heard it except for the fact that Tessa was over and we were microwaving some popcorn in the kitchen.

"Mom, your phone is ringing," I yelled to her upstairs. Dad and I always called that line Mom's phone—it was easier than having to say "the Sarah line" or mentioning Sarah's name at all, something we all tried to avoid whenever possible. Besides, most of the calls had nothing to do with Sarah at this point—she had been gone so many years. The calls Mom got now were mostly invitations to speak at conferences or consultations with the parents of other missing kids. Mom was so good at it, she was in demand, but unless they were somewhat local, she turned them down—she didn't want to leave her family, specifically me, for any length of time.

Tessa opened the fridge and scowled. "Yogurt, more yogurt, and . . . Greek yogurt. Oh, I see some celery. Awesome, so glad I came over."

I poured the popcorn from the bag into a bowl and offered it to her. "What's wrong with this?"

She half smiled and took a handful. "Not as satisfying as chocolate brownie ice cream, which we actually have at my house. Besides, we just played tennis for an hour and a half, I've earned it."

"*I* played tennis, *you* sort of ran around and chased balls, then sat down and had a Gatorade."

Tessa grabbed the popcorn bowl from my hands in mock anger and stomped away with it to the den, spilling kernels along the way. As we walked by Mom's office, I could hear her talking quietly on the phone, something about *how long had she been there?* Another missing kid, I thought to myself, and had to push the emotions that threatened to overwhelm me to the back of my mind, where I stored all the memories of Sarah, of the hurt our family had been through.

Tessa cozied in on the couch and I grabbed the remote. We were watching a Mexican soap opera for school and trying our best to translate the Spanish, with somewhat disastrous results, mostly because we couldn't stop giggling and repeating phrases to each other in mock sexy voices. Actually, the show was pretty good and, while neither of us probably wanted to admit it, we were digging the story line about the handsome stepson and his father's new young bride.

We were arguing about a slang verb conjugation when Mom came and stood in the doorway of the den. I muted the TV and looked up, expecting her to ask us what we wanted for dinner. She had a curious look on her face. "I've just had the oddest call," she began, then hesitated, looking over at Tessa, "from a children's shelter in Florida."

"*Cómo?*" I joked. Tessa shoved my shoulder. "What did they say?"

"Well, they have a girl there. She says her name is Sarah Morris."

When Mom said Sarah's whole name, I felt a shiver run through my body. "Children's shelter?" I repeated. "Sarah would be nineteen now, hardly a child." I aimed the remote at the TV and turned the sound back on, wishing Mom would leave. I didn't want to talk about Sarah, not now.

Mom shrugged and disappeared back into her office, and I heard the printer running a few minutes later. She came back into the den and sat next to me, showing me a printed photo without a word. The image was in color, of a girl with light eyes and blond hair. Her hair was lank and hung on either side of her face, her eyes looked tired, her skin was broken out, her lips chapped and thin. There was beauty there, though weathered, older than the Sarah we'd known. I clicked the TV off and sat up, my hands shaking as I took the photo from Mom.

"Nico, you okay?" Tessa asked, moving closer and looking over my shoulder. "Who is that?"

Mom let out a little laugh. "She *says* she's Sarah Morris."

We all sat silently for a moment, just looking at the photo. The girl was the right age. She looked about twenty, maybe older. I stared into the eyes in the photo, but they were flat, unreadable. Cold.

"Should I call your father?"

Mom knew that Dad hated to be bothered at work with every lead. I took another look at the image . . . something about her eyes.

They were so blank, so empty. More brown than green now. What could do that to a person?

"Yeah, you should call him," I finally managed to mumble. "Because I think this is her."

SARAH

THERE WERE SOME GOOD days, some okay days, in the beginning. And I still think that if I had been better at the rules, if I could have just been *good*, like they wanted me to be, maybe it wouldn't have all gone wrong. But the day I woke up and the door was still locked, I didn't know what to do. They told me to be *quiet, or else*. But I needed to go to the bathroom. So badly. I knocked on the door from the inside, quietly. "Hello?"

An hour went by, maybe more. Or maybe less. When you have to go, it's all you can think about. I tried walking around. Sitting. Lying. I knocked on the door, louder this time. "Please! I have to go to the bathroom." *Quiet. Or else.*

The day went on and on and no one came. No food. No water. And still, I had to go.

Then I cried, another rule broken. *No crying.* I looked at the small pink plastic garbage can in the corner. I looked at it and looked at it and then I couldn't wait anymore. I took the can and used it as a toilet. And oh! The relief. I felt like I could live again, like it would be all right. Even if they left me here, even if I had no food.

I went to put the can back in the corner, but then I saw there was a little hole in the bottom, just big enough. And everything was leaking out, just like a little river. I didn't know how to stop it. So I took off my nightgown and I put it under the can. The nightgown just got all wet, and the pee kept running down and down out of the can until it was almost empty, and all the pee was on the night-gown that was on the rug in the corner.

I took the nightgown, wet and dripping, and shoved it deep under the bed, against the wall. And then I sat and looked out the window as hours and hours went by. I was in just my underwear when they finally opened the door. It had been a whole other day, I was so tired and hungry, and I needed water so badly.

"What the hell is that . . ." He looked around, angry, sniff-ing. "What did you do?" He grabbed my arm and dragged me off the bed, across the rug that ripped at my skin, while I cried and screamed. He hit me. "You're a dirty girl, a bad girl!" And what started as a slap turned worse, turned so bad I wished I'd never been born. *No crying. How many times do I have to tell you?*

After that, it seemed like he had decided about me, that I was bad and could never be good. I never had a second chance. I couldn't stop crying. No matter how hard I tried. I had failed, and I would always be bad in his eyes. And bad girls had to be punished. There were rules, *didn't you know that?* There had to be rules.

CHAPTER 4

I CLOSED MY EYES on the flight, just for a moment, but found myself drifting into a light dreamscape. None of us had slept last night, not really. This morning we left early for the airport for our flight to Florida. The Center for Missing Children had arranged all the details. It was as if our lives had been in slow motion for the past few years, and now everything was happening all at once.

The detectives came over just hours after Mom got the call and the photo. Then Mom's friends from the center. Everyone was pacing around, taking over different rooms, talking on their phones. A flight was arranged. A car at the airport. The detectives spoke with the doctor at the children's shelter in Florida. More photos were sent. More questions. Did Sarah ever break her arm? No. Did she have burns on her back? No. Did she have a scar under her chin? Yes, yes, she did! Yay for the scar under the chin! From falling off the monkey bars at school when she was five. I could tell my parents were so afraid to hope, afraid that with every question this was going to unravel like so many other leads had.

Something felt really different this time, especially when we woke to find a news truck parked outside our house. They hadn't been around in years, not since the early days of Sarah's disappearance. And even then, the media had seemed a little halfhearted, questioning whether this fifteen-year-old girl was a runaway or a victim. They had lingered for a day or two, then vanished as quickly as they had come. Now, as we walked out to Detective Donally's car, they swarmed in with cameras. Mom and Dad pointedly ignored one reporter as she asked, "Do you think you've finally found your daughter, after four years? Is it her? Why do you believe it's her?" I glanced at the woman, her face caked in thick makeup, black liner around her eyes. She probably had to do that for the camera, but it made her appear witchy, her face tight and intense. "Where has she been? Do you know anything about who abducted her?" She never took her eyes off Mom, even when the cameraman switched off the bright light on his camera and lowered it to his side, watching us drive away.

In the car on the way to the airport, Detective Donally went over everything, handing Mom a folder. "Don't be too disturbed by what you see in there," he cautioned, turning around in his seat. "Some of those injuries the doctor asked about may have been sustained while, uh, she was . . ." He trailed off as my mind went to the list of things my sister never had: cigarette burns on her arms and back. Broken bones. Missing teeth. The Sarah we lost had had a scar under her chin, but otherwise she had been perfect. If this girl really was her, she was coming back altered, broken.

In the car, there had been a lot to review. The detective wasn't coming with us—we were on our own until we touched down in Florida—so he told us what we could expect, something about a type of amnesia, how to act when we saw her. I listened, but only halfway. I didn't want to believe anything, not yet. I looked out the window, watching my familiar neighborhood roll by.

After the flurry of the previous afternoon and the ride to the airport, we were quiet on the plane ride. It was just like that day in the car, going to see the body. Would it be her? What if it was her? What if it wasn't?

Mom had taken something, a pill the doctor gave her to calm her nerves, and she collapsed in her seat, still holding Dad's hand tightly, even as she slept with her mouth hanging open. I looked out the window again, my eyes drifting shut, trying not to think about the last day I saw Sarah. How mad she had been. I couldn't play that old movie in my head. Not again. But the memory came anyhow. I had borrowed her gray, soft cashmere sweater without asking. I thought she would never notice. I had put it back into her closet, hung carefully.

"What did you do to my sweater, Nico?" She stood in the doorway of my room, holding the sweater in one hand. It looked limp and shapeless. Had I done that? "Did you tie it around your waist? Yes, you did." She held it up so I could see the sleeves were now somehow too long. "I told you *not* to do that, didn't I?"

I didn't remember her saying that—although she did say I wasn't allowed to borrow any of her clothes.

"You're fat, and when you tie something of mine around your fat waist, it gets all stretched out—got it?" she said.

"I'm not fat," I countered, eyeing her lean frame in my doorway. "Mom says you were the same when you were ten."

"Well, you're not ten. You're almost twelve. And, sorry, but I was never as fat as you. So do me a favor: Stay. The fuck. Out. Of. My. Closet." She stepped forward with each word until she was standing over me. I waited for it: the slap, the shove, for Sarah's eyes to rove around my room and find something precious to me and destroy it. But she kept her eyes locked on mine and didn't move or reach out to hit me.

"Fine," I said, feeling my eyes fill with tears. My weight had been a problem since fourth grade. While I used to be able to wear my sister's old clothes, suddenly, around when I turned nine, they no longer fit. Sarah went through puberty and sprouted up, growing four inches in one year. Her legs went from short and chubby to lean and shapely almost overnight. Her waist cinched in, and hours of cheerleading practice toned everything in all the right places. Her hand-me-down jeans were too tight and too long. The button-up shirts barely closed over my round tummy.

"Sarah was exactly the same way at your age," Mom said, taking me through the plus-size racks at the mall. "Don't even worry about it—you'll get your growth spurt and you'll shoot right up, like Sarah did."

Mom had been right. Of course, the irony was it had happened after Sarah disappeared. I didn't eat—couldn't eat—for what seemed like weeks. And no one slept. Gram came to stay with us then, to help out Mom and Dad. She did the cooking and cleaning, took me to school when I finally went back. She was the one who scraped my full plate into the garbage can every night before doing the dishes, who noticed that my lunch box came back still filled with uneaten sandwiches, cookies, and chips. All the foods I had once loved, the foods that Sarah told me were making me fat, now made me feel sick. Bagels, pizza—the things she denied herself to be thin I now denied myself as if in her memory.

Gram finally took me aside. Held me in front of a mirror, showed me my own face. "You have to eat," she said quietly. "And get some sleep." She patted my shoulder as I looked at myself, what I had become. Sarah had been missing for three months and the weight had slipped away from my face, the roundness of childhood was suddenly gone, and in its place I saw cheekbones. Sarah would be so proud, no longer embarrassed by her fat little sister. I also saw dark purple smears under my eyes, a pale chill on my skin, and a coldness to my expression that hadn't been there before.

In those first weeks, it was Grammie who took me to school every day and, I think, waited outside in her car at the gate until school let out. She was always parked in the same place, a small smile on her face like she was relieved to see me, as if I too might just one day disappear if she didn't keep an eye on me at all times. And then I started to grow—inches, it seemed—overnight, looking more like my missing sister every day. My school uniform pants were too short and too big in the waist, sleeves pulled up to the elbows. Mom was so lost in her world of searching for Sarah she didn't notice.

One night, sitting at the dinner table, while I picked at my salad, she looked over at me and blinked, as if she had seen a ghost. "Have you grown, Nico? Your top doesn't seem to fit."

I shrugged, not wanting to acknowledge that she was right. I had just turned twelve. I needed a bra. I needed new clothes. But somehow admitting that would be wrong—it would mean that months had gone by, it was turning from fall into winter, things were changing, including me. And Sarah was still gone.

Before bed, Mom came into my room, carrying clothes on hangers. It took a moment for my mind to register what they were: Sarah's uniforms, her perfectly pressed navy skirts and tailored white tops with Peter Pan collars and cuffed sleeves. "Why don't you try these until we can take you shopping?"

I said nothing until she was out of the room, then I carefully picked them up. I couldn't help myself, I held the shirt to my face and breathed it in, but there was no scent of Sarah left—not even fabric softener. Then I walked next door to my sister's room and hung the clothes back in her closet, just like they had been before— the skirts all together on one side, shirts on the other. If Sarah came back, I wanted her to know I hadn't touched her things, that I hadn't worn anything, not even her best stuff. I would never make that mistake again.

SARAH

SOMETHING WAS WRONG WITH my arm. Very wrong. It hurt so bad where he twisted and pulled on me, and I couldn't really use my fingers. My face hurt too, but that wasn't so bad. After a day or two, my eye opened back up and I could see again. At night, it would swell up and the headache would come back and I would have to lie on the bed in the dark and be still, very still. I would just listen to them. Fighting, always fighting. And other voices too.

After a few days, I didn't want to complain, but my arm just wasn't working and when I moved it, I hurt so much I felt like I might throw up. When she saw what he had done, she was so angry. "What happened to her arm?"

"I dunno—maybe she fell down or something, she's clumsy."

"Goddamnit, now we have to take her to a doctor—her arm's broke, you stupid shit!"

Then the arguing. That went on for hours, it seemed like. It was night when she came back. She wrapped up my arm tight in a bandage. Then she tied a scarf around my neck and made a sling that my arm could rest in. The scarf was pink and soft. "Now you'll eat something, won't you? Be a good girl." She gave me a white pill for the hurt and a peanut butter sandwich. The bread was brown and very dry, but I didn't want to make any more trouble, so I ate it and took the pill with the milk. In my dreams, I was back home again, and everything was like it used to be. Even the feel of the soft blanket on the bed was the same, as if I was drifting back in time, back to that place, where I was little and I felt safe. As if I could.

CHAPTER 5

I HAD NEVER SAID the words *I love you* to Sarah. And I was pretty sure she had never said them to me. We weren't a family like that. There were not abundant hugs and cuddling on the couch, like I had seen at friends' houses. There was an occasional light hug from Mom, maybe just a loose wrap of arms around your body after a tennis match or getting a lead role in the school play. But usually it was a shoulder squeeze or a hand on the back to say *good job* or *you are loved*.

As we were ushered down the linoleum-lined hallway of the children's shelter, lit overhead by bluish fluorescents, this was all I could think about: How would my parents greet this person? Would they embrace her? Would I be expected to hug her, this girl who looked like my sister but who I had probably never hugged in my entire life. Would we all rush to her and pull her into our arms?

Inside, the building was cool and had a slightly metallic smell, not like the wet heat outside that had hit us the moment we were off the plane. Back home, it was still early spring—damp and green, with clumps of snow melting and plants sprouting everywhere. Here, the air was hot and heavy, and the sun so bright I felt an instant headache the moment I walked outside the airport. I had never been to Florida before.

I wanted to believe it was just the heat, the humidity, that made me feel light-headed. My fingers were tingling and my mouth was dry and felt pasty. Once at the shelter, we were again taken to a nondescript office, almost like at the police station, and asked to sit in green vinyl chairs and wait.

Mom and Dad were silent until I turned to Mom and confessed, "I don't feel good." Then she jumped into action.

"What's wrong? You feel sick, like, to your stomach?" She put her hand on my forehead, my neck.

I shook my head. "I just feel funny, a headache, sort of, but . . ." I put my hand to my stomach. I couldn't put the feeling into words. Fear? Nausea?

"It's probably a migraine, you know I get them all the time." Mom opened her purse and I could see the file from the detective tucked in there. The sight of it made bile rise up my throat. What were we doing here? What was about to happen?

Mom took a small brown prescription bottle out of her bag and opened it.

"Don't give her one of those," Dad murmured, shaking his head. I thought about his Scotch bottle, in the den on the drinks cart. The first thing he did every night when he got home was put down his briefcase and pour himself a drink.

"Just a half." Mom tipped a broken white pill from the bottle and handed it to me. I swallowed it, dry, just as there was a quick knock on the door behind us. We all turned, startled, expecting to look up and see her—Sarah in her cheer uniform, her thick blond hair braided in a side pony, squinting at us with that look on her face: *What are* you *doing here?* as if we were an embarrassment to her.

But it wasn't Sarah; it was a tall woman in a gray dress, holding yet another file in her hands. She sat at the desk across from us and introduced herself. "You must be the Morris family. I wanted to review a few things. . . ." She opened the file.

Mom seemed to vibrate, crossing and uncrossing her legs, adjusting her purse, first on one side, then the floor, then the back of the chair. She had been waiting almost four years, now this delay? This conversation? Couldn't we just see her, talk later?

"Sarah has what we believe is a type of amnesia called retrograde amnesia," the woman explained. "Her memory loss could also be from a TBI—a traumatic brain injury—or simple lack of nutrition. We have not had a chance to run an MRI on her here, but I recommend that you do that, as soon as you get her home. . . . It could give you some answers." She passed Mom a few papers from her file.

Lack of nutrition. Brain injury. The words washed over me and my stomach lurched. I could feel the scratchy trail of the pill down my dry throat. I swallowed hard, willing it to work, to make me feel better somehow.

"Can we just see her now?" Mom asked. I glanced over at her and noticed that her hair was all flattened in back, still messed up from sleeping on the plane, but the pills seemed to have worn off. She was rubbing her hands together and leaning forward in her seat as if she were about to bite this nice woman on the face. "Please."

"Of course, I know how anxious you are," the woman replied, and I could see Mom's blood start to boil. There was no way this woman could have any idea how anxious we were. None. "I just wanted you to be prepared, so that you aren't too disappointed. What I'm trying to say is, Sarah may not recognize you. She knows her name, but she's . . ." Here she trailed off, shaking her head in a sad way.

"Please, can we just see her, we've come all this way." Dad finally spoke, surprising us all.

The woman put her hands on the desk and stood up, nodding to the men by the door. We were led down the hallway, taking every measured step. I saw Mom clasp Dad's hand without a word. We stopped outside a closed door, and, with a quick knock, one of the men swung it open. And just like that, a room appeared, a sunny room with a cot in one corner and a sink and a little desk, a room for a child. And on the simple pink bedspread sat a teenager, all angles and straight dirty-blond hair that fell to her shoulders. She wore a white tank top and a pair of jeans, cheap plastic flip-flops.

The girl looked up. She was so thin, sitting like a little girl, but her skin and expression showed that she was older. Was she nineteen, or was she thirty? It was hard to tell: her face was pale and drawn, skin pulled tight over bones. She looked like Sarah, but in disguise.

Her eyes skipped over me. "Mom?" she said quietly.

I tried to hear, in that one word, if she sounded like Sarah, and then realized, with an awful jolt, that I no longer remembered what Sarah sounded like. What she had sounded like. Before.

"Sarah!" Mom cried. She pushed past me into the room, falling beside the girl and wrapping her arms around her waist. I looked over to Dad and saw what looked like tears on his face.

"My God," he said. "It's her, it's really her." He shook his head and moved to embrace Sarah too as I stood in the doorway, hearing his words over and over again in my head: *It's her. It's her. It's really her.*

CHAPTER 6

"ARE YOU TRAVELING ALONE?" the flight attendant asked. I glanced up at her, then shook my head. "Those are my parents and my, um . . ." I trailed off. I couldn't say it. I couldn't say the word.

"We're together," Dad said. They hadn't thought to book four seats on the return flight, so this was the only way we could all travel home together from Florida. The shelter had released Sarah to my parents with no DNA tests, no fingerprints—she was over the age of eighteen, an adult, and could leave at any time, with anyone she wanted. Now she sat between Mom and Dad, and I was a row ahead and a few seats over.

Sarah. It felt weird to even think her name connected to an actual person. I was used to *Sarah* meaning an empty spot, a blank space, a bottomless pit of anger and hurt.

The flight attendant glanced at my parents, probably wondering why their older daughter sat between them while I sat alone, but of course she couldn't know. Sarah also looked a bit rumpled and worn, in the same clothes she'd had on at the shelter. Mom gave her a sweater to wear over her tank top.

The last time I saw Sarah, she was wearing her white sleeveless dress. It had been a favorite all that summer. She'd dressed it up for her date with a brown leather belt, worn loose around her hips, and she'd paired it with slouchy brown suede boots. It was the day she'd yelled at me for borrowing her gray sweater.

Later, I was so thankful that she had come into my room, stood over me as I lay on the bed, curled up with my paperback romance novel. Screamed at me. Told me I was fat. Because otherwise, when the police asked "What was she wearing?" we wouldn't have been able to answer.

I knew where she was going too: to meet Max at the park. The summer had not been easy for them. First our parents forbade Sarah to date him, then Max's parents also decided things were getting too serious, too fast. But no one could seem to keep them apart; they were constantly finding ways around the rules, meeting at other people's houses, skipping school to be together. Finally, our parents relented and let Sarah see Max, on the condition that she complete her summer school sessions with a tutor. But Max's parents stepped in and put an end to Sarah's hot summer plans: they sent Max away to work as a counselor at a camp in Maine for two months, saying he needed to earn money for college. Worse: there were no phones or internet access allowed at the camp. Sarah stormed around the house with a gray cloud over her head, the only bright spot an occasional letter or postcard from Camp Cumberland. Then, finally, in late August, he was back and Sarah was dying to see him.

"Can't I blow off Mr. Page for once?" Sarah had pleaded the night before at dinner. "I haven't seen Max all summer and he's about to leave for school."

Sarah usually got what she wanted, and what she wanted now was to skip her weekly session with her summer tutor. Without twenty-four hours' notice, I knew he would charge for the missed session, and it wasn't cheap—I had heard enough grumbling from Dad about how much Mr. Page's tutoring cost. Mom glanced at Dad across the table, and his mouth was set in a firm line. "Your junior year is around the corner, you've got to be ready. This is serious, Sarah. Your grades this year mean college—"

Sarah finished his sentence for him. "And college means the rest of your life, I know, I've got it. But I've been going three hours *every* week, all summer. I did what you guys said. Come on." She tilted her head and met his eyes.

Dad relented. "A compromise." He looked over at Mom, getting a nod of approval from her, as if they had already discussed this. "If you promise to study for a few hours here at home, we'll cancel Mr.

Page. Then you can go to the park and meet your friend." It was not lost on anyone that Dad pointedly referred to Max as Sarah's "friend" and not her boyfriend.

A smile spread across Sarah's face—too fast, because Dad kept talking. "But you can't leave Nico here by herself, so you'll have to take her too." He stabbed a tomato on his plate and ate it like he hadn't just dropped a bomb on us.

As Sarah took in this news, I could feel the icy chill of her anger move across the table. Her eyes landed on me, but I just focused on my plate, moving salad and pasta around.

"Are you kidding me? I can't take her—she's . . ." Sarah stopped herself just in time. *She's what?* I wanted to ask. Fat. Not cool. A sixth grader. A loser. An embarrassment. There were so many words she could use to fill the blank.

"Nico's only eleven, and I'm just not comfortable with her being here alone all day," Mom chimed in. "Part of our agreement was that you would look out for her this summer."

"Yeah, but you didn't say I would have to let her ruin my entire life! I've taken her everywhere with me. I'm done."

"Hyperbole," Dad intoned, reaching for the bread.

I knew what they were doing, and Sarah did too. We weren't stupid. If I went with Sarah, there wouldn't be anything "inappropriate" going on between Sarah and her eighteen-year-old boyfriend. I was a de facto chaperone, at age eleven.

Sarah stood suddenly, even though we weren't allowed to leave the table without permission. "Fine, then I won't go. If I have to take Nico, forget it."

Mom and Dad finished their dinner in silence. I hated the scratching sounds of the forks and knives on the plates, with no words spoken. We could hear Sarah's door slam upstairs, then her moving around in her room. Finally, Mom said, "You know she's not mad at you, right? She's mad at us."

Mom and Dad exchanged another look, and I knew they would continue talking about this later—how to handle Sarah. How to keep her calm. It was all they ever talked about. Sarah.

"I'm okay to be here by myself," I said, even though I really wasn't. After an hour or two in the house alone, I usually got spooked by something: the mailman ringing the doorbell, a weird hang-up phone call. One time, Mom had left the dryer in the basement on wrinkle guard, which meant it went on by itself every fifteen minutes. Sarah was home with me then, and I went to her, not daring to enter her room but standing in the doorway to tell her that I'd heard something downstairs. She grabbed one of her cheer batons from the closet before heading into the basement to see what was going on. I cowered at the top of the stairs, waiting for her to come back up.

"Sarah? What is it?" I called down timidly. Of course she pretended not to hear me for the longest time. When she finally came back up, she put her finger to her lips, telling me to stay quiet. "What? What is it?" I asked anxiously, terrified that there was someone—or something—waiting for us in the dark corners. She came up the stairs quietly, then slammed the basement door behind her and locked it, looking over at me with big eyes.

"Nico . . ." she said, her voice shaking.

"What?" I could feel a cold wave wash over me. I was ready to run. We were about to be murdered, like on reality news shows.

"It's . . . it's the . . . *dryer!*" She burst out laughing. "Oh man, Nico, you should see your stupid face right now! I need my phone, I've got to get a picture of this—did you just pee your pants?"

When Mom came home I told her what had happened, how scared I had been, but she brushed it off. Just Sarah being silly, a joke. But—not so funny—Mom remembered it, and ever since then she brought it up as a sign that I wasn't old enough to be left home by myself. Like now. "Nico, remember what happened when the dryer was on wrinkle guard," she said, standing and clearing Sarah's plate with her own.

"That was, like, last year," I pointed out.

Mom acted as if she didn't hear me. "If Sarah really wants to meet Max, she'll take you along. And I think she wants to see him. She'll calm down."

But the next morning, she hadn't calmed down. She didn't speak to me for hours after Mom and Dad left for work. Then she came in with the sweater, the one I had worn and stretched. She stormed out, slamming my door behind her, more chips of paint cracking from the doorframe. I still didn't know if I was going with her or not. About an hour before she was supposed to meet Max, she was still home primping, leaning in to the bathroom mirror with a mascara wand. I heard her cell phone ring, then tense words. I thought at first it was Mom checking in, but then I heard Sarah call the person a "fucking bitch," and I knew that even Sarah wouldn't say that to our parents. When they checked her phone records later, at that exact time Paula had called. Her best friend. Her former best friend.

Waiting for her in my room, I put on what I thought was an okay outfit for hanging out with high school kids: jean shorts and a black tank top. I was going to wear something else, a T-shirt that had the name of my middle school tennis team on it, but I knew Sarah would make me change. *Your team came in third place this season. If that was my shirt, I'd burn it.* I pulled my hair up into a ponytail and sat on my bed, reading a paperback from the library until Sarah was ready. But Sarah never came back in my room that morning. Moments later, I heard the garage door open, the *tick-tick-tick* of her bike wheels below my window, then the garage closing as she rode off.

When the cops kept asking us where she was supposed to be, or where people had seen her last, my parents could only vaguely tell them MacArthur, a vast park that spread for over five miles on the edge of our suburb. It was only about a mile from where we lived, easy to bike to. It didn't really matter, though, because when they interviewed Max, it turned out that she had never made it past the bike racks. No one had seen her. He had waited for over an hour, calling her cell about ten times.

So it was easy to figure out who was the last person to see Sarah. It was me.

And I knew right away to keep my mouth shut about what she had said to me. I almost told the detective, as he sat at our kitchen table. He seemed so warm and so relaxed, calmly asking questions while Mom sat wringing her hands. "Did your sister seem anxious or upset about anything that day?" he asked.

Sarah's angry face flashed through my mind. She leaned over me where I sat on my bed, cowering. She held the stretched-out sweater in one hand, but her other hand was free. Free to hit, free to slap. I knew she could make me sorry. I answered the detective: "No, she seemed fine."

"How about her tutor, Mr. Page, do you know him?" Mr. Page was a grandfather's age, a retired high school chemistry teacher.

"I don't know him," I had to admit. "But he seems really nice."

"Was Sarah excited to go meet her, uh, friend?" I noticed he looked down at the notebook in his hand as if to check their names one more time. "Did she mention anyone she was having a problem with—another boy, maybe, or a female friend?" He tapped the list with his pen.

I shook my head. Sarah would kill me if I told them about the situation with Paula and Max. Besides, that wasn't really a problem, it was just how Sarah operated. Paula had liked Max, had had a crush on him for over a year. And Sarah got him. She won. Plain and simple. If Paula was mad about it, or jealous—"tough titties." That's what Sarah would say. Like when they both went out for cheerleading and Sarah got on the A-squad. She had worked for it, it was earned. And she would be right, but I knew it still hurt Paula that Sarah was always a little bit better. A little thinner, her hair a little blonder and longer, her cheer jumps a little higher. It wasn't fair, but it's just how things were. Until Max.

"Would you like something to drink?" The flight attendant leaned over my seat, pulling me from my memories.

"I'm okay," I answered, turning to look back at my parents, and

Sarah, as she raised a glass of something to her lips. Orange juice. Sarah said orange juice gave her cankers. That it was full of empty calories. But maybe she had outgrown that. I guess she had. Or her amnesia made her forget. She seemed to remember us, our names and our faces, but we hadn't asked too many questions at the shelter. Mom and Dad were just anxious to get her home again. To have Sarah, their daughter, back.

Before I could stop myself, I flipped up my tray table as soon as the drinks cart moved by me and headed down the aisle. I leaned over their seats and said quietly, "Sarah, orange juice gives you cankers. You might not want to drink that." I nodded to her half-empty glass.

Mom instantly shot me a look full of daggers, but Sarah kept her eyes down, her face an unhealthy pale, saying nothing. I walked on numb legs to the bathroom and slid the door lock behind me. I leaned against the wall and looked into the mirror, seeing only Sarah's old face looking back at me.

SARAH

THE NEXT TIME, IT wasn't really my fault. She had yelled at him for hurting my arm, and he was mad about it. So he decided to break her rules. He let me out, just for a little bit, just to watch TV with him while she was gone. It was my first time out of the room except to use the bathroom. And even then, they would watch me. "Come sit with me," he told me. "A little closer." It wasn't like a question, so I did what he said.

My arm was still in a sling. He touched it gently and asked me, "That hurt?" I shook my head and he cracked a smile. I could tell I had made him happy and then I just wanted to see that smile again, to know that I was doing the right things. If I was *good*, I wouldn't get hurt again.

I guess he saw my eyes looking at the door, at all the locks there. He put his cigarette out. "Don't even think about trying to run off—that arm is nothing compared to what you'll get." He took off his white T-shirt, stretching it over his head. His chest had lots of hair and, under that, tattoos marked his skin. I sat with him and did everything he told me to do until he heard her car in the driveway and then he said to run, run back into the room, and I better not say a goddamn thing or I would be so goddamn sorry.

The door locked behind me. When I heard the voices later, they sounded happy. They forgot to bring me anything for dinner, but that was okay. I was happy—as happy as I could be in the small room with the dark window. I thought the hurting had stopped. But I was wrong.

CHAPTER 7

THERE WOULD BE NO interviews, no media. My parents decided that right away. Sarah was too fragile, she needed to see doctors. And that wasn't the only reason. The detectives in Florida had told us something terrifying: Whoever had taken Sarah might not have let her go. She might have escaped. If she had, they might come back for her—worried that she would remember. Worried that she was only pretending she had amnesia. They told us we weren't allowed to say anything to anyone, even family, about her ordeal and what she could (or couldn't) remember. This suited Mom perfectly. "Our family is our priority, not *People* magazine," I heard her say into her cell on the drive home. We rode in a black SUV on the way home from the airport, Mom next to Sarah while Dad and I sat in the back.

"A press release is fine, as long as I have approval over it, but I really don't want reporters and media calling the house or coming by," she explained. "How can we keep our address out of print?" The years that Mom had spent helping others to get their children back were coming in handy now: training for how to handle everything that might come our way.

Sarah looked out the window at the scenery rolling by and I tried to see it through her eyes. As we left the city and came into Mapleview, the suburbs sprawled. Golf courses, playgrounds, and parks surrounded by turn-of-the-century homes on streets with names like Spring Oak and Fern Dell.

When finally the car pulled to a stop in front of our gray-and-white house, she moved to the door and looked out at the carefully manicured lawn, up at the second floor. "Do you remember this?" Dad asked cautiously.

Sarah nodded, her lank blond hair bobbing. She had barely spoken since we'd left the shelter, but now she offered up one word, "yes," in a whisper.

The news van was gone and, while I didn't quite know how Mom had managed it, there were no reporters waiting in the bushes for us. We simply got out of the car and went into the house. Once inside, the three of us stood and watched as Sarah moved, silently, through each room, laying her hands on things and looking out the windows. Mom couldn't help herself and had to ask, "Do you remember this? How about this? Any of this look familiar?"

In the front room, she stopped at the piano and slowly picked up a framed photo of our family—the one that had been used on the news after Sarah went missing. "I remember that dress," she said, running her hands over the image.

"You do? Oh, that's so great." Mom practically clapped and Dad was beaming. I tried to see our home as she must see it now. Two floors, spacious and decorated with Mom's flair for beautiful antiques. The money to live in this neighborhood hadn't come just from Dad's work, though he made tons. Some of it was from Mom's family too—she had grown up this way. I looked around at all the nice things we had, the beauty of our home that I took for granted. The den with a surround sound system, the kitchen full of expensive appliances and chef's oven. What the counselor had said about Sarah being starved floated into my head as I watched her run her fingers over the fruit bowl on the marble counter—apples and pears, carefully polished. They weren't really ever eaten, not by us anyhow. The cleaning lady just shined them up and replaced them when they went soft.

"Would you like something to eat?" Mom asked.

Sarah nodded, her eyes still darting around the room until Dad said, "Let's sit down."

Sarah pulled out the chair closest to her and sat down at the table while we all froze for a moment. That was my seat. Sarah's chair was on the other side of the table, Mom and Dad on either end. That's how it always had been since Sarah and I were little.

"Well, um, Nico, why don't you sit here?" Dad said, pulling out the chair on the other side. The chair that had been empty for four years: Sarah's chair.

I sat down with a stiff back, as if I didn't really want the chair to touch me, while Mom busied herself at the counter, putting together a sandwich for Sarah. "We don't have the kind of cheese you like," she said, almost talking to herself.

"Anything's fine, really," Sarah said quietly, that slight southern twang drifting into her voice, something that hadn't been there before. When Mom slid the sandwich in front of her, I held my breath, waiting for the old Sarah to show up. *Swiss cheese? Really? It smells like sick, I can't eat this.* Or: *Is this turkey the low-sodium kind? You know I can't bloat, we've got a game on Saturday.*

But this girl just sat and ate the sandwich in big bites, chewing with her mouth slightly open and murmuring, saying "So good" between bites. I tried not to stare, but I couldn't take my eyes off her face as she ate.

When you see an old friend or a relative who you haven't seen in a while—maybe over summer break or a few months or a year even—and then you see them again, it's the little things you pick up on. What's different from how you picture them in your mind.

How you last saw them. And at first, it's jarring. Maybe they gained weight, like my uncle Phil did one year, and when we saw him again, Dad said he looked like someone had taken an air pump and stuck it up his butt and gave it a few hard pumps. Sarah and I had a good laugh about that, and it was true. He looked the same, just like Uncle Phil, but inflated somehow.

As I looked at Sarah now, all I could think of was how *def*lated she looked. Hair hung limp to her shoulders, brittle and too yellow, her face was thin and pale. Her eyes seemed to have fewer lashes. I studied her hands on the sandwich. Her nails were smaller, bitten down and ragged, cuticles torn.

To be fair, I looked different too, now so much taller and thinner. I wasn't the chubby little eleven-year-old sister Sarah had last seen, with braces and a forehead covered in pimples.

She glanced up from her plate and took a long drink of water. Dad said, "Well, that disappeared awful fast. You want another one?"

Mom was in the kitchen already fixing more sandwiches. "It's no problem at all, I've got one right here."

Sarah caught my eye and I flinched, waiting for her to snarl, *What are you staring at?* Instead she gave me a small, sincere smile and nodded. "Sure, I'll take another one."

CHAPTER 8

IT WAS ALMOST A relief when the detectives showed up later. I used to dread them coming to the house. I would actually hide out in my room or the den when I saw their unmarked Ford pull into our driveway. But today, the sound of the bell was so welcome, I raced to the door to get it—anything to get away from the table and my family just sitting there looking at one another.

I let in Detective Donally and Detective Spencer before my parents could reach the door, but I could hear Mom complain, "They didn't say they were coming today."

"Maybe they're just here to keep reporters away, you did ask for that," Dad pointed out.

As soon as the men were in the house, Dad came to shake hands. He led them into the kitchen, murmuring under his breath about the amnesia and how tired Sarah was. I stood in the archway to the kitchen and watched.

"Sarah, I'm Detective Donally, this is my partner, Detective Spencer; we're with the state police. We sure are glad to see you home, safe and sound. The children's shelter in Florida is sending us over some files as well, just to follow up on your release." He pulled out a chair and motioned to my mom as if asking permission before sitting down.

Mom nodded, but said quickly, "We've just gotten home and were having something to eat, I think Sarah might need time to rest." She wiped her hands on a dish towel. "Can I offer you a cup of coffee or anything? I'm afraid I only have instant."

Donally shook his head. "Oh, no worries, we won't be long, just wanted to check in and introduce ourselves. Set up a time for Sarah to come down to the station for a talk." He undid his jacket and I could see the black gun strapped to his belt.

"Why does she need to come to the station?" Dad asked. He went to stand behind Sarah's chair while Detective Spencer circled the table and stood on the other side, looking around the kitchen. He was always the quiet one, letting Detective Donally do the talking.

"Well, because she's a crime victim and we need to talk to her about that crime." He smiled over at Dad as if he was talking to a child.

"She can't remember anything. We're going to take her for an MRI to see . . . to see why." Mom caught herself before saying what they mentioned at the shelter—the possibility that Sarah had brain damage.

"We'll still need to ask her some questions—that okay with you, Sarah?" Detective Donally asked.

Sarah met his eyes warmly and nodded. "Sure."

Everyone else in the room seemed to let out a sigh. We were all waiting to see how Sarah would react, how she would handle questioning. None of us had asked her yet what she remembered, as if we were hoping it was all a blank and things could just go back to how they were. But now that wouldn't be possible, the police had to have their answers: Where had she been these past four years? Was she kidnapped? If so, who was responsible? I wasn't sure my parents really wanted the answers.

"Why don't we pick you up about nine tomorrow morning, okay?" Donally asked, standing and buttoning his jacket over his gun.

"We can just bring her over," Mom said quickly.

"You don't need to bother. Sarah's an adult now, isn't that right? You're eighteen now?" Detective Donally asked her.

Sarah looked over at me in the doorway as if I held the answer, not at Mom or Dad.

"Her birthday is in March," I said. The memory of Sarah's birthday, the actual date, the dread of that day, of what we had done on her birthdays while she was missing, caught in my throat as I added, "She just turned nineteen."

Sarah nodded. "March eleventh," she said mechanically. "That's my birthday."

"Well, look at that, she does remember some things." Donally gave Sarah a tight smile and pushed his chair in. "She won't need you all to come in with her. But if you want to send your lawyer, that's fine." Before Mom could respond, he turned back to Sarah. "See you tomorrow, Sarah, and welcome home."

Dad shot Mom a look behind the detective's back as he went to walk them to the door. When he came back into the kitchen, Mom and I were still silent. "Why would she need a lawyer there?" I asked.

"I'm sure it's just how they do things," Mom said cautiously. "Sarah, if you're not ready for this . . ." The way she said Sarah's name hung in the air.

"It's okay," Sarah said, again a little lilt of the South in her voice. "I just don't know how much I can help them." She was so quiet, she sounded like a little girl.

"I'm sure you're anxious to see your room and get some rest," Mom offered, starting to lead her back through the front of the house to the stairs. When Sarah walked into her room, I held my breath, waiting for her to jump on the bed or run to her closet, so happy to be home. But she looked around as if she had never seen the place before. She moved across the carpet to the bulletin board by her mirror. She fingered the silky cheerleading award ribbons and glanced at the photos pinned there as if searching for something she knew.

"Max," she said, pointing to one. "And Polly . . . no, Paula?"

"That's right, your friends," Mom said. "Do you recognize anyone else?"

Sarah looked closely at the images. "Sort of, but not really. It's like it's right here"—she pointed to the front of her head—"but I can't get at it."

"Might be because you need these." I laughed, handing her the glasses on her desk. She only wore them at school and for reading, but I wondered if she even remembered them.

"I wear glasses?" she asked, looking confused. They were light purple frames and went great with her blond hair.

"Just sometimes, like to see the board at school," Mom explained.

She put them on and squinted at the photos again, stepping back, clearly unable to see anything. Her prescription had obviously changed over the past four years, and she didn't even know it.

I looked over at Dad, standing in the doorway, and saw a sad look cross his face. His daughter was home, his little girl, but she wasn't really Sarah—not anymore.

SARAH

I HAD BEEN IN the room for two days with nothing to eat. This time, he had a special treat for me: a package of two cupcakes wrapped up in cellophane. Chocolate cupcakes with a white swirl on the top.

"You say anything to her? You tell her anything?" he asked me. He held the cupcakes just out of my reach.

I shook my head. Of course I didn't say anything to her. Why would I? This was our special time, when she was gone and he was supposed to be gone too but he was here and watching TV.

Sometimes when she came back and I was in the room, I could hear her asking him, "Why'd you smoke all my cigarettes?" or "Where's the beer?" And then I was nervous that she would know what he had done. But he always had an answer for her and then they would laugh and I would hear music and voices all into the night. I knew I must be doing good, because no one had hurt me in a long time.

CHAPTER 9

THE NEXT MORNING, SARAH was up early, just like me and Mom. The Curse of the Morris Women, Mom called it—we always woke early. Sarah had never needed an alarm clock, and this morning was no exception. She came out of her room wearing the same dirty clothes from the shelter: jeans and a white tank top with Mom's borrowed sweater over them. She was even wearing the grubby flip-flops.

"Don't you think you want to wear something else today, at least some warmer shoes?" Mom asked, serving us toasted bagels.

"These are fine," Sarah said quickly. But Mom headed up the stairs to Sarah's room, talking to herself. I looked over at Sarah and realized it was the first moment we had been alone together since yesterday, since she'd come home. The first time in four years. I found it hard to take my eyes off her face: sharp, pointy angles I didn't recognize as "Sarah" yet. I waited for her to speak, to say my name the way she used to, drawn out, like when she was angry with me. *So, Nee-co . . .*

But she didn't say anything, instead she seemed totally focused on eating her bagel as quickly as possible, like someone might come and snatch it away from her.

"You, uh, sleep okay?" I asked, breaking the awkward silence, then felt stupid. That was a question for a guest, not for your sister. And also, how could she sleep? She had a back covered in cigarette burns and didn't know where she had been for four years—no one with a past like that could possibly close their eyes and feel safe ever again.

"Yeah," she said quietly. She looked up at me with an open expression on her face that I didn't recognize at all. "But I'd kill for some coffee—do you guys have any?"

You guys.

"I think Mom might have some around." I stood up to check the cabinets. "You know, when Gram comes she likes it." I found instant coffee and held it out to her, raising my eyebrows.

"Better than nothing." She smiled. "They'll have some real stuff at the station—you know how cops love their coffee."

She picked up a second bagel and I put the kettle on the stove, wondering how Sarah knew that cops loved coffee. Mom had offered it to the detectives yesterday.

Mom came back in with an armful of clothes. "Maybe this?"

She held up a black dress, but Sarah just shook her head. "This?" She showed us a tailored wool jacket. "At least cover your feet, it's chilly out." She put a pair of leather ballet flats beside Sarah. "Why is the stove on?"

"I'm making some coffee, for Sarah," I said, and Mom looked over at me quizzically. I watched as Sarah slipped off her flip-flops and put her feet into the flats, or tried to. They were too small, and she pulled at the back to try and cram her toes in.

The doorbell sounded and Mom left the kitchen to get the door just as Sarah stood up. I brought her the coffee mug. "Those fit okay?" I asked, motioning down to the shoes. The front was crammed with her toes, shoved in like one of Cinderella's step-sisters'.

"They're a little tight," she admitted. "You know, if you don't wear leather shoes for a while, sometimes they shrink up."

"I'll grab you a pair of mine—hold on," I told her. I could hear Mom talking to the detectives on the porch as I raced up the stairs. I wore a size 8 now; Sarah had been a size 7 before. I walked by Sarah's room, and stood outside the closed door for a moment. Should I grab another pair from her closet for her? Maybe she was right about them shrinking. A minute later, I came down with a pair of flats from my own closet.

Sarah took them gratefully and pulled them on fast, swigging coffee from the mug in front of her—black, no sugar. "These are perfect. Here goes nothing, huh?" She smiled at me as she headed for the door.

Mom had convinced the detectives to let Dad accompany Sarah, so we watched from the front yard as they drove off all together in an unmarked police car. I learned to recognize these cars early on after Sarah's disappearance, when they were parked outside our house most days: dark blue or black Ford four-door sedans with no registration sticker on the plates.

"I almost don't want to let her out of my sight, you know?" Mom admitted. She wrapped her arms around herself and looked on the verge of tears.

I knew how she felt. The night before, I had been tempted to steal into Sarah's room, just to look at her asleep, just to check that there was a real girl in Sarah's bed.

"You know, her shoes—" I started to say, then stopped myself.

"What about her shoes?" Mom asked.

"Nothing, just that they don't fit anymore." I kicked the frosty dew off some blades of grass as we went back up the walk to the house.

"I was thinking that we need to take her shopping. I'm sure all her old stuff doesn't fit, and frankly I don't want to see her in any of those clothes. It would be like seeing a ghost."

I thought of Sarah's beautiful clothes—a closet full, untouched, unworn, the clothes I had once coveted. The clothes that Mom had preserved for the past four years, hanging neatly in her closet, the room kept just as it had been when Sarah was fifteen, waiting for her. Now it was all out of style, wouldn't fit, wouldn't work for the Sarah who had come back to us.

The last time I'd been in the room was when Tessa stayed over one night after Christmas break. I hadn't wanted to go in there; I never did. But Tessa wanted to see. We'd been best friends for three years, but still, she had never known Sarah. She met me as "the girl whose sister disappeared" and had become friends with me knowing only that. Of course her parents knew the whole story, and at first they wouldn't let Tessa come over to spend the night. I guess they were worried someone might come back for me—or one of my friends. Whoever took Sarah. Or, if Sarah ran away, there was always the question of her influence on me. Was my sister bad? Was I too?

There was a dark cloud over me, over our whole family. But slowly, as the years passed with no leads and no news about Sarah, most people in town, and most of the parents at school, forgot. We were no longer *that family* with the missing daughter. Other scandals replaced ours—a single mom having an affair with the married PE teacher, or the pretty teacher's aide who had a secret porn background. Sarah's disappearance seemed less tawdry and salacious than those stories. And I proved myself to be good, reliable, not a runaway, not a bad girl. Sarah's disappearance was not our fault—Mom always reminded me of that. It was not something we had done; it was something that had happened to us. She was the one to call Tessa's parents and get their permission for the sleepover—my first since Sarah's disappearance.

Tessa and I had been up late, in my room, trying to take some good photos on my phone. They were supposed to look casual—oh, hey, just hanging out at my friend's house—but also cute and somewhat sexy. The plan was to post one or two on Tessa's Instagram. We knew her crush, Liam, had been checking and making comments, so the pics were really for him. But we would never admit it, especially because he already had a girlfriend in our class, Kelly.

I'd done Tessa's makeup and styled her hair, but still the pics weren't anything fabulous. She threw open the doors to my closet and let out a sigh. "You've got like five hundred uniform tops in here and nothing else. Don't you ever wear anything but a uniform?"

I shrugged, not willing to admit that I actually liked the navy skirts and white tops that we wore for school. It made getting dressed really easy; I didn't have to think. I had a few pairs of jeans and T-shirts for the weekend and some summer dresses, but not a lot else. I never could figure out how to put cool outfits together, so I just stuck with simple. *Nico, you look like you got your clothes out of the lost and found bin at school. Mom, please don't let her go out like that.*

Tessa pushed the hangers to one side and looked at what was left—a couple of sundresses and jackets. "What about your mom or your sister—do you think they might have anything? I mean, just to wear for the pictures," Tessa added quickly.

I didn't know how to respond. Next door was a room full of beautiful things—shoes, sunglasses, jewelry, clothing. All carefully selected by Sarah, who wouldn't settle for anything but the best. She created outfits based on images torn from magazines. She was the one in the family who appreciated fashion—in fact, Mom often said that she was going to grow up to be a designer. Before she disappeared, she had taken a sewing class at school and made a few things—a dress and a sleeveless top—and had easily gotten an A+, the teacher noting that she had a real talent for "line," whatever that meant.

"I'm sorry, that was . . . I don't know what's wrong with me." Tessa sat next to me on my bed. "Nico?"

I stared off into space, suddenly coming around. "No, it's okay. You're right. Sarah has all kinds of stuff that's just sitting in there, we might as well use it."

"You sure?" Tessa looked reluctant now, scared even.

I nodded and opened the door to the dark hallway—my parents had been asleep for hours. We walked to the room next door and I turned the knob, opening it, probably for the first time in months. But when I flipped on the light switch it was clear that nothing inside had changed. Everything was just as Sarah had left it that morning, or at least how the detectives left it after they had gone through everything. The room even smelled like Sarah still, of the perfume she wore when she started dating Max. The cleaning lady came in to dust sometimes, but otherwise the room was untouched.

Tessa moved to the bulletin board covered with awards and ribbons. "Wow, impressive." She fingered one of the cheer awards. "Cheerleader extraordinaire, huh?"

"She did gymnastics and dance too," I pointed out. I didn't want her to think that Sarah was just a cheerleader. She was so much more. She was good at everything she did. Not just good—the best.

Tessa moved to the double doors of the closet and swung them open, looking over the dresses and tops that hung there, carefully arranged by color. "Wow—even more impressive!" She pulled out a pale pink top and held it up to her chin, moving over to the mirror to see herself. "This is beautiful—what do you think?"

I could only nod, seeing my best friend with her curly dark hair holding Sarah's pink shirt. It was a beautiful color for Tessa.

She should have it. I knew she should, but part of me, deep inside, screamed: *No. Don't. Put it back.*

"What was she like, your sister? I mean, I get that she was really good at school and cheer and everything." Tessa walked back over to the board, looking now at the photos of Sarah and her friends that were pinned there. She leaned in to look at one closely, of Sarah and Paula. "But what was she *really* like?"

I stood in Sarah's room and looked at all her perfect things that went with her perfect life. She was perfect, I wanted to say. She was beautiful and smart. She always won. She always got what she wanted.

"She was awful," I said. "She was really awful."

CHAPTER 10

WHEN WE CAME BACK into the house, Mom reminded me that later in the day, a counselor from the Center for Missing Children would be over to meet with us. "Just to help us all get used to this. It's a lot to handle." She delivered the news with a sense of glee and lightness in her voice as she cleaned up the kitchen from breakfast. She lifted Sarah's coffee mug from the table and cradled it in her hands for a moment, gazing at it as if she didn't know if she should put it in a museum or into the dishwasher.

The last time we'd had a counselor over, it was to help us deal with Sarah's disappearance. He had come over every day at first, then once a week, and then the sessions stopped. Those were dark days for me, for all three of us. I didn't remember a lot of it. How we got through it. I remember being told I had to eat, and Mom's doctor giving her some pills that she shared with me so that I could sleep. The nightmares were terrible. But, like everything else, those stopped too. Now we would be meeting a counselor under very different circumstances, and I could tell that Mom was thrilled to be a success story—to need help welcoming her daughter back into the family instead of dealing with a devastating loss.

"Tessa is going to bring by your homework assignments this afternoon, but I think Monday is soon enough to go back to school, don't you?" Mom asked.

I nodded and picked up a bite of bagel that was left on my plate, eating it before Mom could clear it from the table.

Mom touched my arm and looked into my eyes. "I know it's a lot, Nico, all of it. Sarah being gone, Sarah being back. I don't want you to ever think that Daddy and I have lost sight of what's important in all of this. Of how important you are to us. You and Sarah."

"Mom, I know." I shrugged. We didn't have a lot of heart-to-heart emotional talks in our family—it made me uncomfortable.

"I mean it, Nico, I really mean it. The past few years have been hard on you—on all of us." She hesitated. "Sometimes I think we didn't handle Sarah's disappearance right."

When she said that, I shook my head. What was the "right" way to deal? What did she think she had done wrong?

Mom went on. "I know you suffered, we all did. I just . . ." She stopped for a moment before finishing her thought. "I want to handle her return right—does that make sense?"

I nodded, noticing tears brimming in her eyes. Suddenly, she smiled.

"It is going to take some time. It's all just so strange, every little thing, I mean, look—I'm doing breakfast dishes for two girls, my girls—" She broke down, her face crumpling in before she turned her back to me and busied herself at the sink. "I'm so happy to be doing just the ordinary things, the simplest things." She let out a light laugh. "I know I'm a silly woman."

"No, I get it," I agreed, thinking of how good it felt to make Sarah a cup of coffee, to grab her a pair of shoes. "I do."

I went upstairs to my room, where I noticed my closet was still open. I pushed the door shut, thinking about how Sarah was, right now, at the police station, wearing my shoes. It gave me such an odd feeling, like I was connected to her somehow.

I went into the hallway and stood outside her door for a moment, the room that had been empty for four years. I turned the knob and went in, noticing first that she had carefully made the bed. Neat, as always, everything in its place.

On the bedside table was a book from Sarah's shelf: *Rebecca* by Daphne du Maurier, one of Sarah's favorites. She had made us all watch the old black-and-white movie years ago when she was working on a book report. The story was dull and forgettable— something about a guy who had killed his wife because she was cheating on him. That was the big reveal. Sarah had read the book several times, and now it looked like she was reading it again.

I moved to the desk and opened a few drawers, finding everything the same as it had been for years. The closet too was untouched. I looked at Sarah's shoe rack, trying to decide if Mom had given her the flats from here or from her own closet, but it was hard to tell. I hadn't memorized every pair of shoes in the closet and where they went, but now I found myself wishing I had.

Why?

I ran my hands over the desk, finding nothing, not even dust there. What was I looking for in this room? I turned and caught my reflection in the mirror over the dressing table: the very image of Sarah when she went missing.

I knew what I was looking for, even if I didn't want to admit it to myself. I was looking for something that would prove to me that this girl really was Sarah, that this stranger was my sister.

SARAH

SOME NIGHTS I WOULD lie on that bed in the dark and stare at the ceiling, thinking about food. I wasn't missing anyone or anything, or wanting to go home again—I just wanted something to eat. I thought about fried chicken and mashed potatoes. And fast food, like French fries. My stomach hurt so bad, I felt like it was turning inside out. Sometimes I would drift off to sleep and wake up grinding my teeth, thinking about eating.

One of my teeth, a big one, got loose and wiggled around and I was scared it was because of my dreams and thinking about eating too much. Every day I put my fingers on it and moved it around more and more until one awful day the tooth just totally fell out. Right out into my hand, covered in blood and spit. I sat there and cried for what must have been hours and then I fell asleep with the bloody tooth in my hand and blood on my pillowcase.

When she came into the room with a tray like she did some days,

I sat up and she saw the blood. "What have you done now?" she said, and I had to show her even though I didn't want to. I opened my hand and she saw the tooth and she just laughed.

"You're such a crybaby, everybody loses a tooth now and then. That's nothing to cry about." Then she left me there with the dried brown blood on my hand and a small plate of food to eat: some pretzels and yellow cheese in plastic wrappers and a soda that was warm and a weird flavor. But I ate it all; I just chewed on the other side.

CHAPTER 11

BY THE TIME DAD and Sarah were done with the police interview, the news media had also somehow gotten the word. Mom called Dad's cell and left a message to pull straight into the garage when they came home, that the cameras and vans were waiting outside. I knew what she was trying to avoid—and what they all wanted: a photo of how Sarah looked now, and Mom was not about to let them have it.

At Mom's request, the detectives had sent over a couple of uniformed cops, who kept the reporters off the lawn, but they hovered on the sidewalk, where their shouts could be heard as Detective Donally's car turned into the driveway. I watched from my bedroom window as Mom pushed the button to open the garage and he pulled in, the door quickly sliding down behind him as the reporters called out, "Who took you, Sarah? Did you run away?" and "Where have you been?" "Were you kidnapped?" "Did they hurt you?"

I went downstairs as soon as I heard them come in, but Detective Donally never even got out of the car. When he pulled out of the garage a few moments later, the yelling started again. The reporters couldn't see into the car's tinted windows and followed the car out of the driveway, microphones in hand, cameras at the ready, trying to catch a glimpse of whoever was inside.

I rounded the corner into the kitchen to see Sarah standing there next to Dad. She looked up at me and met my eyes, and for a moment, it was as if she didn't know me. I got that same sick feeling I'd had at the shelter in Florida, tingling and numb, a whooshing sound in my ears as my heart beat hard. *What did she tell them?*

Then she smiled, like she was actually happy to be home, to see me. Relieved. I searched Dad's face, looking for an answer to the questions I didn't dare ask. We all stood there, unsure of what to do next.

"So?" Mom finally said.

"Well, she tried, but she couldn't give them a lot," Dad said. "I don't really know why they insisted on questioning someone with amnesia, seems like a waste of time to me."

Even though it was early afternoon, Dad moved into the den, leaving the three of us in the kitchen, and I heard the sound of his glass clinking against the bottle as he poured himself a drink. By the time the counselor from the Center for Missing Children arrived at the front door, under another intense attack from reporters, Dad was already on his third.

More answers about Sarah's visit to the police came out during our first home counseling session. Sarah hadn't been able to tell the detectives anything. She didn't know where she had been or what had happened to her—nothing. It was all a blank.

The police had asked about her bike, the one she rode on that last day. It had been found, carefully locked at a bike rack at the entrance to the park, about half a mile from where she was supposed to meet Max. When they dusted it for prints, all they found were Paula's and mine (aside from Sarah's, which were expected). But those were easily explained; I might have moved Sarah's bike in the garage, and Paula said she had borrowed it once or twice. Sarah couldn't remember leaving her bike there, or even where in the park she was meeting her boyfriend.

They asked about Max and showed her photos of her other friends. But most were a blank too—she remembered names, but nothing about them. Who she got along with, who she didn't. If she had been fighting with anyone. Dad said she just shook her head, saying almost nothing.

"Did you run away, or did someone force you?" they asked her. "Were you kept in Florida? How long had you been there?" Her first memory was of waking up on the beach, in the jeans and tank top, with no shoes on. A police officer found her there and took her to the children's shelter. From that point, her memory began again, but everything before that was lost or foggy.

The counselor from the center, an older woman named Dr. Levine, told us not to push Sarah. "The memories will return on their own, or they might not. Sometimes this kind of forgetting is a gift from the brain. It allows us to remember what we can handle and forget the rest."

What the counselor said rang true for me—those first days and weeks after Sarah disappeared, they were all a blur now. What did I eat, what did I wear, what did I say to the detectives? It was like a dream, a terrible dream. My brain, trying not to deal, forgetting what I couldn't face.

The counselor looked from my parents over to Sarah and spoke to her directly. "You might remember some things next week, next year, or maybe even ten years from now," she said. She seemed like a young grandmother and spoke slowly and soothingly. "I had a client who suffered terrible abuse and was only able to recall her childhood when she had a child of her own. And by then, quite honestly, she was older and more stable and able to handle the memories."

There was a moment of silence in the living room until Mom spoke. "What about seeing friends and relatives? Of course everyone wants to come and visit Sarah—Uncle Phil, the cousins, her grandmother—but we don't want to overwhelm her. Would that be pushing things?"

Dr. Levine nodded and wrote something in the notebook on her lap. "That's a good instinct you had there, exactly. It can be very overwhelming to see all these people you are expected to know but can't quite recall."

I looked over to Sarah to see if she had any thoughts to add, but she was just staring at Dr. Levine with a blank expression, slightly bored. Or maybe she was just tired.

"Sarah, do you feel ready to see people—maybe a relative or two? Some old friends?"

She blinked, then quickly answered. "I'm not sure. Maybe, just to see how it goes."

Dr. Levine looked over at Mom. "A welcome-home party is certainly out of the question, as I'm sure you understand." She smiled.

"Max emailed me—he wanted to drive down this weekend. If that's okay," I offered, looking from Sarah to Dr. Levine, trying to gauge their reactions.

"Well, your Gram also wants to come, and I think it's family first," Mom said.

"The answers to all of these questions are right here—with Sarah," Dr. Levine pointed out. "Give her some time to think about what, and who, she's ready to handle, and you'll know when the time is right."

That night, after Dr. Levine left, Sarah went to her room but left the door ajar, so a sliver of light shone into the hallway. I knocked gently and heard her say, "Come on in."

She sat on the bed with the copy of *Rebecca* in her hands. It looked like she was reading it really slowly, for some reason—the bookmark had hardly moved. "That's one of your favorite books, you know. You've read it a bunch of times."

"Really? I'm loving it so much. But I don't remember ever reading it before," she admitted. She let out a little laugh. "The story does seem familiar, now that you mention it."

"I guess that's one good thing about amnesia, you can redo all kinds of stuff—books and movies, roller coasters . . ." As soon as the words were out of my mouth, I felt weird for joking about it. I looked at her face to be sure I hadn't offended her. She pulled in her legs and patted the end of the bed, inviting me to sit down. I hesitated. I had never sat on her bed in my life.

"Sit," she finally insisted, tilting her head to one side.

"Naw, I'm sure you're tired, I really just wanted to say good night." I moved to the door.

"Nico?"

I met her eyes, suddenly having a terrible feeling she was going to say something like, *Don't ever come in my room again.*

"Can you leave the door a little bit open? I don't like to be closed in."

"Sure." It was hard to believe this was the same Sarah who had always insisted on privacy, who had a habit of slamming her door, hard, behind anyone foolish enough to leave it open. As I left, I dimmed the hallway light, then I went into my own room and closed the door behind me.

That night, I woke to the sound of screaming. *"Let me out!"* I jerked awake, my feet on the floor before I even knew where I was. In a moment I was at Sarah's door, panting for breath. *"Stop, stop!"* she yelled.

Dad stood in the hallway, in the dim light, and whispered to me, "It's okay, Sarah's just having a nightmare, go back to bed." I peered into Sarah's room and saw Mom on the bed next to her, holding her and rocking her back and forth as she sobbed and gulped air.

"It's okay, you're home now, you're safe, you're okay," Mom said over and over again.

"Nico, back to bed," Dad commanded.

Before I turned back into my room, I whispered to him, "Leave the door open a little, she doesn't like it closed."

He looked at me with sad eyes and rubbed the stubble on his face. "I know," he said.

I went back into my room and lay in bed, just staring at the ceiling. I heard Dad go downstairs and hit some buttons on the panel for the alarm system next to the front door, probably checking to be sure it was armed and the door securely locked. I could hear him pacing, his slippers on the hardwood floor, checking the windows and doors, like he sometimes did before we went on vacation. But I wasn't sure who he was protecting us from. The damage had already been done.

SARAH

THERE WAS ONE BOOK in the room, oversized with a puffy front cover, like there was padding inside it. It was white and felt like leather to the touch. It was an illustrated book of Bible stories for kids, big pictures with everything from Adam and Eve to Moses parting the Red Sea.

They never said I could look at the book, so I only did it in secret, when I was alone in the room for a long time. When I heard the key in the lock, I would quick put it back.

The next time I got in trouble, I thought it was maybe because I had been looking at the book. But that wasn't why. It happened because she washed some clothes that had been sitting around. I only had two or three things to wear then and I just wore them over and over.

She said she saw something. "Has he been messing with you?" she asked me, and I didn't know what to say so I just shook my head.

She sat on the bed and looked at me for a long time, then pulled the blanket up around my shoulders and tucked me in. She had never done anything nice like that before.

That night, the yelling was so bad I could hear it even though I pressed my hands hard over my ears. If only they had neighbors, they would hear and call the police, but from what I had seen out the little window, we were too far away for anyone to know what was happening. I couldn't see another house or car anywhere. I just sat on the bed and rocked and rocked for hours. Sometimes I would get out that old Bible book and look at the pictures, but not now. There was noise and yelling and things being thrown. It was not a time for Bible pictures.

CHAPTER 12

MAX AND GRAM WEREN'T the only ones who wanted to see Sarah. My friends were all dying to come over, suddenly, and everyone wanted a photo of how she looked now. She had been gone for four years—was she still the same pretty girl? Or had she been tarnished in some way that could never wash off? Even Tessa, who stopped by with my assignments from school and lingered in the doorway, her mom's car idling in our driveway.

"Can I stay for a little bit? Mom said I can, if your mom says it's okay," she said breathlessly, looking past my shoulder. I couldn't help but think back to just a year or two before, when Tessa hadn't even been allowed to come over or spend the night. Now we were suddenly celebrities, and everyone wanted a piece of us.

"It's not a good idea," I said, though I didn't fault her. I wanted her to come in so we could talk—really talk—about what was going on. Tessa would know what to do.

"We saw on the news—she really doesn't remember anything? I mean, like, nothing?"

I nodded. "Yeah, she's reading a book right now that she read before, and she doesn't even remember that." As soon as the words were out of my mouth, I felt I had betrayed my family, my sister. Mom and Dad had been very clear: no media, and no talking to anyone about Sarah. We didn't know how the facts about her having amnesia had gotten out, but Mom suspected it was a leak from the children's shelter in Florida. We hadn't released anything: no photos, though the papers and magazines had been clamoring for them. Mom had fielded calls from news shows like *48 Hours* and *Dateline* and also magazines—even *People*. But she turned everyone down.

"I want to give other people hope, the families of missing children—to tell them to keep believing and that maybe it will happen for them too, but not at the expense of my own daughter's mental health." That was the statement she gave to most sources.

"Can I see her?" Tessa whispered, leaning in, and I had to shake my head.

"Don't even tell anybody what I said about the book, okay?"

Tessa nodded seriously. "Okay." She lingered for a moment. "You know Liam is having that party tomorrow night? I feel weird going without you."

"That's okay, you should just go," I said, taking the pile of books from her hands.

"So you don't think your parents will let you? My mom will drive us."

I looked out at Tessa's mom in the car. She was usually on her phone, but not today. She was watching us, waiting to see if Tessa was going to get inside. If I was going to come out. If Sarah was going to make an appearance.

"I dunno, I have to see." Really I knew that we already had plans for the weekend. Max was coming into town, but I couldn't tell Tessa that.

"Okay, well . . ." Tessa met my eyes. "I guess just let me know, okay?"

I felt a weird detachment from her, as if I was lying to her. We usually told each other everything. I didn't like how it felt to keep secrets from my best friend—if that's what I was doing.

After the family session with Dr. Levine, we talked about visitors and let Sarah decide who she wanted to see first. She had agreed to let Max come for a visit over the weekend, but she was nervous—not about her amnesia, but about something else. At dinner Friday night, she said quietly, "I'm mostly just worried what people will think of how I look now."

"What is that supposed to mean?" Mom laughed lightly. But I knew what Sarah meant. She could see from the photos all over the house how she used to look. And she didn't look like that anymore.

Sarah sighed and stared down at her plate. She didn't want to say the words. "They might think I'm different now. Ugly."

"You are not ugly, Sarah," Mom was quick to say. "You are a beautiful girl, and I want you to see that. Whatever it takes to make you feel better, we're going to do it, right, Nico?" Mom looked over at me.

"Yeah, of course," I agreed. But Sarah was right. Max was going to be shocked to see her—older, so thin and drawn. That glow, that whole "Sarah" thing, was gone, and I didn't know how she could possibly get it back.

"How about this? Tomorrow, before Max comes over, we go see Amanda at the salon—makeovers all around. Then shopping—you need new clothes, shoes, everything. Okay?"

Sarah smiled. "I'd like that," she said, taking a bite of pasta from her plate. "I love this pasta."

"It's gnocchi," I told her. "Your favorite, but you almost never ate it because you said it had too many calories."

"Nico!" Mom snapped.

"What? It's true, she used to say that."

Dad pushed his plate away. "Well, it's mighty filling, I'll give you that."

Actually, what Sarah used to say was that I shouldn't eat pasta, because I was so fat already. *I wish we could order pizza, but Nico can't have any*, she told her friends who were over one night. *My mom had to put her fat ass on a diet, so now we all have to suffer. Thanks, Nico.*

I looked over at Sarah now and tried to marry her words from the past with this person sitting at the table. She smiled at me and took another bite, this washed-out version of my sister. Deep down, part of me still hated her, even though I knew that was wrong. I had tried so hard after she was gone. Tried to remember only the good things about her, but it was nearly impossible.

On her birthday every year, Mom and Dad left white roses at the entrance to MacArthur Park, and they made me come, too. March 11, early spring, and almost always raining or damp. A dozen white roses, wrapped in a yellow ribbon, wasted, left to rot on the brick wall at the entrance arch. We never actually set foot in the park, just stood outside the gates. Mom made us each say something— something good we remembered about Sarah. The first year, I said something about how she was so awesome at cheer. That was easy, a good thing, a true thing. The next year, I mentioned how she always kept her room so neat. Mom had laughed at that, through her tears.

And this year, just a month ago, it was easier for me to say something nice about Sarah as the memory of her cruelty faded. I was more forgiving. I said she always wanted the best for me, which was true, sort of. She wanted me to be thin and pretty like her; she wanted me to care about my appearance, to work out instead of constantly reading. To have more friends, be more popular. All the things that had happened for me after Sarah went away. Without Sarah's shadow over me, I became what she wanted me to be. And now she was back. But that didn't mean that I had forgotten.

CHAPTER 13

THE NEXT DAY, WE left the house with Sarah bundled up in a hat, sunglasses, and baggy clothes. If anyone was waiting outside with a camera, they would be disappointed. But I didn't see any of the news media trucks that had parked outside those first few days. Perhaps they had moved on, forgotten us already, or the police presence had finally intimidated them into leaving. I noticed just one car that looked a little suspicious, probably an unmarked police car, but I didn't get a good look at the plates as Mom drove out of the garage.

Mom checked the rearview mirror a few times on the drive, but saw nothing. And I knew that Amanda—her longtime stylist—had emptied the salon for us that morning. Amanda had actually done Sarah's hair before, just a trim now and then, or for a big dance at school.

When we got to the salon, Amanda, a tiny woman with short

spiky black hair and a light British accent, raced toward us and hugged us all, saving Sarah for last. I saw tears in her eyes as she held her. "You sit right here, we're taking care of you first, guest of honor," she told Sarah, wrapping a cape over her clothes as she sat down. Mom and I sat on either side and Amanda's assistant started on Mom's trim.

Amanda fluffed up Sarah's lank tresses. "Looks like it's just a little overprocessed . . ." she murmured, then caught herself. "Nothing that can't be fixed." She smiled and pulled a comb carefully through Sarah's hair, parting it. "That's your real color right there, sort of a light brown." She pointed at the roots. "I've been coloring your mom's hair for years"—she leaned in and whispered—"and that's her real color exactly. Now, how blond do you want to go?"

"Well, Nico has the most beautiful hair. I'd love to have her color, if you can even get close to it," Sarah said. She smiled over at me and I felt my neck get hot and red with embarrassment. I couldn't remember a time when Sarah had given me a compliment. To call my hair beautiful—I was shocked.

"You'd be surprised what I can do, a few highlights and low-lights." She combed through Sarah's hair carefully. "You'll have to lose a couple of inches to damage, but otherwise, you'll look like twins."

Sarah reached over and took my hand as Amanda started working on her hair, and our eyes met in the mirror. Her smile was sincere, relieved, happy. Feeling the small bones of her hand as she squeezed mine, I had to smile back.

Two hours later, we left the salon looking more like a family: all the same shade of blond and trimmed and styled to perfection. Sarah's hair was a few inches shorter now, just above her shoulders, but the color was amazing: We did look like twins, just like Amanda had promised.

"Lunch at the mall, then shopping?" Mom said as we headed for the car. Sarah slipped on her sunglasses and, with her newly lightened hair, looked better than she had in days.

"I'm starving, and I think I'm in the mood to go shopping. How about you, Nico?" she asked me. It was probably her longest sentence since she got home.

I looked over at her, almost too stunned to answer. Was she really asking me how I felt, what I wanted to do—instead of just insisting we do what she wanted? "Yeah, sure, why not," I said, climbing into the backseat. Sarah took the seat beside me instead of sitting up front.

"I feel like we used to do this all the time," Sarah said, pulling on her seat belt. "Shop together, right?"

At first I thought she was being sarcastic, old Sarah, back with the digs. But there was no laugh, no *as if!* We never went shopping together. She always went with her friends, and I just didn't go. I looked down at my boyfriend-cut jeans and old concert tee. An outfit that Sarah would have called "dumpy." *No way is Nico coming with us, we aren't going to the store for fatties—oh, I mean plus-size. Isn't that where you get your clothes, Nico?*

Sarah kept her sunglasses on at the mall, but I wasn't sure she really needed to—the place was mobbed, and I felt like no one took any notice of two blond teens and their mom eating subs at the food court or popping into boutiques. When anyone did do a double take at us, I reminded myself that there hadn't been any photos of Sarah since she returned, and Mom looked so different from the old press photos they were using, no one would recognize her.

After Sarah went missing, for a few months at least, we couldn't go anywhere without people coming up to us. They just wanted to say how sorry they were, or that they had seen us on the news. Once, at the grocery store, a teenage boy bagging Mom's groceries asked, "Aren't you that family where the girl ran away? Whatever happened to her?" Mom completely dissolved into tears, sobbing so loudly the manager had to come and walk us out to the car. After that, every time someone recognized us as "the family of that girl," I felt my anxiety meter creep up. I didn't want anyone to say something stupid or in haste that would hurt Mom or Dad, but usually they were just sympathetic and kind. Still, it was one benefit of the passage of years—people forget, someone else's story replaces yours on the front page, and you just go on with your life.

We went into a couple of stores, but Sarah didn't find much that she liked. "Too preppy," she'd say, passing up racks of outfits that she would have pounced on a few years ago. She finally picked out a couple of pairs of jeans and a few casual tops to try on. Some of the stuff looked more like nightclub wear than clothes for everyday, but Mom wasn't saying no to anything.

When we went to the dressing rooms, Sarah linked arms with me and almost pulled me in with her. "I'll wait out here," I said, uncomfortable with her new physical displays of affection.

"'Kay," she said, closing the door behind her. "I'll only show you the stuff I think looks decent."

She opened the door a minute later, coming out in a bright printed top and skinny jeans that revealed how thin her legs had become. The top had a T-back and showed off her slender shoulders, the bones knobby under the skin.

"What do you think?" She was facing me but I could see in the mirror behind her the circle of a pink burn on her shoulder blade. I knew she had lots of small burns on her back from the report that Mom was given, but I hadn't seen one before. Now that I did—the spot where someone had pressed a burning cigarette into her fragile skin—I caught my breath.

"What?" Sarah said, whirling around to look in the mirror.

"You have—you can see—"

Sarah turned around and looked at the reflection of her shoulder. "Oh." She scowled. "Too bad, it's a cute top from the front."

Before thinking, I reached out and put my fingers gently on the scar. It felt soft and smooth, almost plastic. "Does it hurt?" I asked.

Sarah shook her head. "It was a long time ago," she said, stripping off the top and dropping it on the floor.

I registered what she had said before she did: *A long time ago.* How long? I thought she couldn't remember.

When she saw my face in the mirror she caught herself. "I mean, it has to be, right?" She smiled, slipping another top over her head.

It was a long time ago. The words kept ringing in my head. Did Sarah remember more than she was telling us?

"Nico, is this one too tight, you think?" she asked me now. Our eyes met in the mirror. "Come on, be honest." Suddenly the smile left her face and she added, in a low tone, "You know you can be totally honest with me." We stood like that for a moment, neither of us saying anything, an electricity between us that I didn't fully understand.

Then Sarah smiled her earnest smile, something that I still wasn't used to. The Sarah of my memory had a downturned mouth, unless she was with her friends or with Max. "You could pull this off.

Why don't you try it?" she added, unbuttoning the top. And that was perhaps the most jarring thing of all: her niceness. Her sweet way with me. How she reached for my hand at the salon. Her open heart, her love. Gone were the sarcasm, the biting insults. I had almost stopped bracing for acid comments every time she opened her mouth. Almost.

I looked at her in the mirror, thin and washed out, even with her expensive new color and cut. The fitted pink top making her skin look even paler, her body smaller. This girl was broken and scarred. Something horrible had happened to her, that was certain. Somehow, she had come out of it, survived, and become the person she was now—someone wonderful. But she wasn't my sister.

SARAH

HE BURNED ME THE next day. In the morning, he opened the door and came in while I was asleep. I felt his weight on the bed next to me and I rolled over. He smelled like old beer and cigarettes and sweat. He was smoking and didn't look at me. Just said, "You fucked up real good this time, kid."

I didn't know if he was talking to me or to himself.

When he looked over at me, he said, "Don't give me that face." Then he reached over and pressed his cigarette onto my back. At first I didn't know what was happening, then I felt it all at once, right through my nightgown, a sting and burn and sizzle. I jerked away, and quick, he was on me, holding me down, my face into the pillow with his arm on the back of my neck. And another burn and another. I screamed but the pillow filled my mouth. I couldn't hear myself screaming, even in my own ears. He pressed harder on me and I couldn't breathe.

Then he burned me again and I felt myself drifting from the pain. It didn't hurt anymore because I was just floating up, like there was a big wave under me, carrying me far. Carrying me far.

CHAPTER 14

I GOT THROUGH THE afternoon of shopping, woodenly saying "yes" or "no" to items she picked out—clothes my real sister would never wear, fabrics she would never let touch her body. When we walked back through the atrium to the parking lot, she suddenly stopped, shying away from a guy who bumped her accidentally. "Sorry," he said under his breath, and kept going. Mom put her arm around Sarah's waist and guided her to the door as I walked behind them, trying to make sure no one else came too close.

We got home without any problems—no one following us, no news crews outside. I could tell Mom was relieved as she pulled the car into the garage. If she had her way, Sarah would never leave the house again. When we got into the kitchen, Sarah took one look at the clock and her face blanched. "I've only got an hour before he gets here?"

"You look wonderful, what's wrong?" Mom asked.

Sarah rolled her eyes, exasperated with Mom, and I thought I saw a glimpse of something, the old Sarah. *You don't get it, none of you.* Maybe I just wanted to see it, to convince myself.

"Nico, you've got to help me." Sarah raced upstairs, carrying her bags of new clothes.

I followed her into her room, where she dropped the bags on the floor. Sarah sat in front of the mirror and dumped out her old makeup bag, poking through it. "This stuff . . ." She shook her head and started to say something, then caught herself. I saw her pick up the metal eyelash curler and set it to one side. The rest of the old makeup—eye shadow, powder, lip stain—she pushed off the side of the table with the back of her hand into the garbage.

She pulled over a small white bag and started unpacking the new products Mom had just bought at the department store: a really expensive face cream, foundation, eyeliner, and lipstick. All of it came in fancy-looking boxes, which she lined up on the side of the dressing table, her eyes as big as a kid's on Christmas morning. "Well, it's showtime." She opened the lotion and smoothed it over her face carefully as I watched, noting the small pocks where pimples must have left scars. "Maybe this stuff will do the trick."

This stuff will do the trick. Sarah would never say that.

"You're in charge of music." She nodded to the speakers on the bookshelf. I pulled my phone from my pocket and plugged it in, scrolling to a playlist. *Nico, I heard you listening to that stupid boy band. What are you, like, seven or something? You really like that crap?*

"Nice," she said, bobbing her head to the first song as it played. I sat on her bed, uneasily, and watched as she expertly applied a thick layer of eyeliner.

"I'm thinking the skinny jeans and the black top, the one that ties up here?" she said. "Can you dig those ones out for me and cut off the tags?"

I did what she asked and laid the clothes on the bed, then started to leave so she could dress, but she stripped off her pants and slid into the new jeans before changing her top, giving me a glimpse of how empty her bra was, stretched over her ribs.

She leaned into the mirror and fluffed up her hair. "You're so quiet—is it because I look terrible?"

"No." I shook my head. She actually looked good, almost like Sarah used to, although with a bit more makeup than she used to wear. "You look really great."

She smiled at herself in the mirror, as if I wasn't there, a perfect imitation of the Sarah pictures on the bulletin board—head tipped down just a bit, eyes narrowed. "Do you think he'll look the same? Just as cute?" She moved over to the photos and studied them closely.

After Sarah went missing, we had been in close contact with

Max for a while. Mom and I had both repeatedly defended him to the cops, making sure they knew that we didn't suspect him, that he couldn't be responsible. He loved Sarah—probably more than we did. Still, they questioned him over and over, searched his house and his family cabin, and they found plenty. Her hair was everywhere. Her fingerprints. Yes, she had been there, but they didn't find what they were looking for: Signs of struggle. Blood.

Just when it seemed like the looming suspicion of guilt had lifted, two years ago, a local paper had done an article about Sarah, looking into her disappearance again. There were photos of Max and Paula. And, of course, the talk started up again. Mom spent a lot of time on the phone with his parents after that article was published. It didn't seem to matter how many times our family gave statements about his innocence or Paula's, people still thought Max had something to do with Sarah's disappearance, probably right up until she returned.

"When was the last time you saw him?" Sarah asked, running her finger over the photo, touching his face.

I had bumped into Max last winter, when he was home for Christmas, shopping downtown. It was startling to see him and we had an awkward hug. Neither of us even said Sarah's name. And he looked just as handsome, if not more.

"Not that long ago, and, yeah, he still looks pretty good,"

I admitted. "You know, he went through a really bad time—" I started to tell her, but then the doorbell rang downstairs.

Sarah turned to me, grabbing my hands. "Oh my God!" We went down the stairs. Dad had already opened the door to Max before we got there, so we saw him standing in the front hall. Tall, dark, and handsome summed it up—now with the broad shoulders of a man to go with it. He turned to look at Sarah. It felt like time stood still as I watched his face, waiting to see his reaction. What would he say? I waited for him to say the words that were running through my head: *That's not Sarah.*

Max stood still, rigid, his jaw muscles tense. He didn't seem to blink, looking at her. The air felt charged with something: electricity, fire, metal, static.

"Wow," he said quietly. Finally, a slow smile. "I didn't want to believe it until I saw you, but just, wow!" He moved to lift her into his arms in a bear hug.

I felt myself breathe—I hadn't realized until that moment that I'd been holding myself rigid, waiting. What was he seeing? I looked at her, the blond hair, the smile, and the clothes. It was Sarah, of course it was Sarah. I thought back to how I had been feeling in the dressing room at the mall, watching her, detached, like she was a stranger. Holding myself apart from her. What was wrong with me?

"You weigh nothing!" he said before he could stop himself. And then, in the doorway, I saw someone else—short dark-blond hair, a black coat. Paula.

"Oh, Paula," Mom said, taking her eyes off Max and Sarah for a moment. "We weren't expecting you—what a nice surprise." I wasn't sure if anyone but me could tell that her tone was decidedly not happy. We all sat in the living room and awkwardly stared at Sarah between conversation and the crudités Mom had set out. My parents asked about college and Max and Paula gave the stock answers about what they were studying.

"We're going to help Sarah take her GED, once she's settled, so maybe she'll be joining you both soon," Mom offered. Sarah's face was unreadable at the news.

Paula sat close to Max, their thighs touching, and put her arm around him as she asked, "Do we look much different to you?"

Sarah smiled a little, then admitted, "Well, Max has a beard now."

Everyone laughed, except Paula, who corrected her. "Not a beard, he just hasn't shaved for a couple of days." She looked over at him and I could feel the affection between them. They had bonded over Sarah's disappearance years ago, but now they seemed to be really in love—at least, Paula was. Max never took his eyes off Sarah.

Sarah's face was somewhat ashen, seeing them together. We

hadn't thought to tell her that Max and Paula had been together for a few years. Mom thought it would be best for Max to tell Sarah himself, but now it was too late.

"Well, you sure look different," Paula said, and when Mom shot her a look she added, "You look great, just older, I mean, we all do, right?" Max looked down at his shoes and rubbed his hands together. She went on talking, awkwardly, as if trying to cover what she had said, bury it under more small talk. "And I cut my hair. Remember? It used to be as long as yours, Nico."

Her last few words hung in the air, as if no one knew what to say next, how to get into a conversation that meant anything. I felt that funny rushing sound in my ears as my heart started to beat fast. I closed my eyes just for a second and willed myself to be calm. *None of this is going to be easy*, the counselor had told us. She was right.

I looked over to Sarah and saw that her mouth was set in a thin line. Part of me wanted to be happy, to see Sarah not get her way—for once. To have Paula sitting there with Max, claiming him as hers. But this wasn't Sarah, even though she looked like her—not the same Sarah from before—this girl did not deserve to be hurt by her friends. The image of that little round scar on her back flashed into my mind.

Mom broke the tension by asking if she could get drinks for everyone. "I'd love a beer, if you've got any," Max said. At first I thought he was joking but then quickly remembered that he was over twenty-one now.

"I'll check. Nico, care to help me?" Mom gave me a look that told me it wasn't really a question.

The moment we got into the kitchen, Mom slammed open the fridge. "Who does that girl think she is to come here—this was supposed to be for Sarah and Max." She moved some bottles around and found one of Dad's beers.

"Mom, they're a couple, they've been together for years."

"Still, she couldn't let Sarah have half an hour with him alone—an hour? That's too much?"

I shrugged. "I'm sure they were so excited to see her that they just didn't think about it. They were all friends, remember?" I said, but my mind kept replaying Paula looking over at Max, that little smug smile on her face. She didn't have to do that.

"You're right," Mom said with a sigh. "I'm just thinking of Sarah—I wish we could make everything like it was for her. But that's not going to happen, is it?"

I shook my head and went to pick up the tray Mom had fixed. What had happened at the mall was still haunting me. *It was a long time ago.* "Don't you think it's weird how she's so . . ." The word wouldn't come to me. "How Sarah's so different now?"

Mom tilted her head. "Different how?"

Was it possible that she hadn't picked up on everything I had, all the things I was seeing? "Just, the clothes she wanted to get, and well . . ." I thought of the other things: her hair being darker, her shoes too small. When I really thought about it, they were all easily explained away. The shoes were Mom's. Or her feet had grown. The hair—someone dyed it an ashy blond, trying to disguise her. All of those little things were not as strange as how she was acting: Nice. Loving. Like a real sister. And how I was feeling about her: Protective. Defensive.

"We all wish our old Sarah was back, that everything was just like before, but this is the Sarah we've got," Mom said. "And I am so happy that I just don't want to compare things to how they were before." She added some ice to the water glasses on the tray. "Yes, she's different. She's older, for one, and we don't know what she's been through. But she's back, she's with us, she's safe, and that's what's important." Mom stopped moving and talking for a moment. She put her hands on her hips and took in a deep breath. I watched as she arranged her tense features into a more pleasant face, a small fake smile replacing the line of her lips.

Her eyes met mine and I knew. Of course she had noticed the differences, all the strange little things that didn't add up. But Sarah was back now, the black hole in our family had been filled. And that was all that mattered.

CHAPTER 15

AFTER PAULA AND MAX left, I helped Mom clear the living room. "Your phone was buzzing," she said to me, fluffing the pillows on the couch. She arranged them so that everything was perfect again, as if the short, awkward visit never happened. "You had a bunch of text messages. Not that I was looking at your phone—it was just in the kitchen."

I put Max's empty beer bottle and Paula's glass on the tray. I knew that Mom checked my phone. She had the pass code, she probably scanned through it every night. I could tell, sometimes, by what had been left open—the photos or my email was the last thing looked at—when I had closed those apps. It didn't bother me because I knew what she was looking for. It wasn't coming from a place of distrust or her concern that I was going to disappear like Sarah had. She wasn't suspicious about secret boyfriends or if I was doing drugs. She and Dad were worried about something else, in the opposite direction: that I wasn't having a normal teen-age life. That I didn't have friends. That I didn't go out, wasn't invited to things. They both worried—well, mostly Mom—that Sarah's disappearance had ruined any chance for me of being a regular teen girl. And while Mom always reminded me that what happened to Sarah wasn't our fault, I know she blamed herself for how they handled it and how much of my life had been lost in that mix.

I brought the tray into the kitchen and picked up my phone, scanning through the text messages from Tessa. Mom came in and started loading the dishwasher. I knew she was dying to ask who the messages were from.

Finally, I broke the suspense. "It's just Tessa, some party tonight . . ." I started to say.

Mom instantly brightened. "Oh, a party? At Tessa's house?"

"It's at Liam's. It's his birthday." I shrugged and leaned back against the counter. I didn't go to many parties. There had been a few, mostly birthday parties where my mom would stay to help out. Only in the past year had she let me go to someone else's house unaccompanied, and that was a big deal. She or Dad had to drive me there and pick me up, checking in with the parents to be sure an adult would be there the whole time. "It's tonight—seems strange to go."

"Why?" Mom closed the dishwasher and turned to face me. "Because of Sarah?"

I didn't say anything, just looked down. "What am I supposed to say to people? It's weird."

Mom nodded. "I understand. But I bet after about five minutes of asking you questions, everyone will drop it and move on. You should go, sweetie." She smiled. "You're back to school Monday anyhow—it might be a good thing to just see everyone and get it over with, right? Plus, you just had your hair done and it looks so good. Don't you want to show it off?"

I couldn't believe that Mom was pushing me to go to a party, practically shoving me. Her sudden desperation for a normal life for not only me but for all of us made me feel a little sorry for her. If I went to the party, it would be for her, not even because I wanted to.

"What about Sarah?"

"She's exhausted, I'm sure—both physically and emotionally. That was a lot today." Mom pulled a frozen lasagna from the fridge and unwrapped it, preheating the oven. "Go on, tell Tessa you can go. Really, Nico, I think you should."

As I went upstairs with my phone in my hand, I realized that maybe she wanted me to go out for another reason—to have some time alone with Sarah. I hadn't considered that. Since Sarah had gotten back, we'd done everything together. Even when Dad wasn't around, I was.

I walked by Sarah's door and noticed that the light was off, even though it was starting to grow dark outside. Maybe she was asleep. I stood outside the door for a moment, listening, but heard nothing.

In my own room, I turned on all the lights and slipped my phone into the speaker, playing a new song Tessa had recommended. I dumped the shopping bag from the mall onto my bed and looked over the stuff I'd picked out—nothing that special: a new pair of skinny jeans in a soft gray that Sarah had proclaimed "awesome" and a simple white T-shirt in a slouchy boyfriend fit. "You can wear a dark bra under, with straps showing," Sarah had offered. It wasn't exactly my style.

I slid off my top and put on the new white shirt, letting the shoulder fall to one side, showing the thin strap of my pink bra. Sarah was right, it looked kind of good. I pulled on the new jeans and added a silver belt. I had only one long necklace—a gift from Tessa for my last birthday, a silver chain with a set of white angel wings dangling from it. I put it around my neck and let it fall long over the soft shirt.

I picked up my phone and texted Tessa back: *When can you pick me up?*

I ate dinner with Mom and Dad, lasagna and a quick salad Mom threw together. Sarah's room was still dark and Mom said not to bother her, to let her sleep if she wanted to. "I think it took a lot out of her, seeing those two," she said, sipping her second glass of wine.

"Maybe she needs some new friends," Dad proclaimed.

"I'd say so," Mom agreed. "Paula—that girl has some problems, serious issues still with Sarah. It's so unhealthy and immature. I mean, considering . . ."

I pushed the food around on my plate, not willing to pile insults onto Paula. They didn't understand, fully, what she had been through with Sarah. How she had been treated. Their complicated history. How strange it must be for her to now be back. I could relate. It didn't excuse Paula's behavior, but it did explain it.

Mom went on: "As if no time had passed, as if Sarah hasn't been through absolute hell. I mean, can you imagine, asking her to go running tomorrow morning? You should have seen Sarah's face."

It was comical, the idea that this thin, anemic version of Sarah would leap from bed tomorrow wanting to run to the track with Paula just like they used to. I thought, for a moment, when Paula suggested the idea of running at the track that Sarah would burst out laughing. But she seemed to consider it carefully, saying instead, shyly, *I'll think about it.*

A car horn sounded from the driveway and we all startled. "That's Tessa." I grabbed my bag and a sweater and headed to the door. "I won't be super late or anything."

Both of their faces turned to me, fragile smiles and eager eyes. "Just have fun, kiddo," Dad said, sounding like a father on a sitcom.

"Call us if you need a ride or anything, anything at all, okay?" Mom looked like she was ready to walk me out to the car and kiss my cheek but held her seat.

"'Kay, bye." I tried to be casual as I closed the door behind me. I could feel their watchful gaze on me as I climbed into the back of Tessa's mom's car. Music was blasting, the heat was on high, and the car smelled of Tessa's fruit-flavored lip gloss.

Tessa threw her arms around me, yanking me to her. "I'm *so* glad you decided to come! This is going to be crazy!"

Her mom turned down the music for a moment and backed the car from the driveway. "How's it going, Nico? We have been thinking about you. Tessa says you didn't make it to school all week."

I took a deep breath and said the words I had been preparing in my head. "It's been pretty strange, but good. We're just really happy to have Sarah home."

"I bet." Tessa's mom met my eyes in the rearview mirror. "How is she?"

I paused, wondering how to answer that. *She's different.* "She's really, really good. Still adjusting, but she's really good."

"Mom! I told you Nico isn't allowed to talk about it. Can you turn this song up?" Tessa rolled her eyes at me and mouthed the word *sorry*.

"It's okay," I said. I looked out the car window at the lights in all the other homes we drove by, the flicker of TV screens. I longed to be sitting in the den at home, with my parents, watching a movie like we usually did on Saturday night. Just the three of us. I wondered if they would be doing that with Sarah tonight.

". . . this could be good or it could be bad, because you know I always thought Alex sort of liked Kelly and acted like he didn't just because she was with Liam, but I guess we'll see tonight, huh?" Tessa was talking but I could barely keep up.

"Wait, when did Kelly and Liam break up?"

"Last week, you were out. I was going to call you, but, I mean, you were dealing with way bigger stuff." Tessa pulled out a lip gloss and smeared it on just as her mom pulled in front of Liam's house. Lights seemed to glow from every window and I could already hear a low bass line of beats escaping from the open front door.

Tessa's mom said quickly, "You know the rules," before unlocking the doors. "Text me when you're ready to be picked up."

"We'll be good, promise. Love you, Mom!" Tessa called as we tumbled out of the back and up the rounded driveway.

"You're almost a foot taller," I had to point out. Tessa, usually tiny, was suddenly statuesque, matching my height.

"New boots." She pointed down to her heels. "They kill! You don't know how lucky you are to be tall."

"Tess, are your feet, like, still growing, or are you the same size?" I asked as we reached the door.

"What?" Tessa pulled a funny face. "I'm a size six, have been for years. Why? Do these make my feet look big?"

I shook my head.

"No, tell me, Nico. Do they? You need to tell me now because I've hardly worn them and I can still take them back . . ."

"They're good." I couldn't tell her the real reason I was asking. "Really."

Tessa looked like she didn't believe me as we went into the foyer and saw a group of kids from school in the living room. I had never been to Liam's house, and was surprised to see how big it was. I knew he was an only child and lived with just his father. What did the two of them do in this place?

"Ladies!" Liam's best friend, Miles, came over and flopped an arm around each of our shoulders. He turned to me. "Very surprised to see you here."

"Leave her alone," Tessa said, sliding out from under his arm.

"Not because of the whole 'kidnapped sister returns' thing, but you just never go to parties," Miles pointed out.

"Whoa." Idina walked by and did a double take. She grabbed

both my hands in hers. "How are you?" She pulled me in for an uncomfortable hug. "I called you a few days ago, but I didn't hear back—and that's totally cool—but, oh my God, Nico!"

"Yeah, I know." I nodded. "Sorry I didn't call you, it's been . . ." I shook my head, suddenly feeling tears in my eyes. *Don't lose it. Don't cry, you fat stupid baby, you always cry about everything.*

"So crazy, everybody has been talking about you, but you're okay? Right? And your sister?"

I took a deep breath and willed myself to stay calm. "Actually, everything is really good. I mean it, like, excellent." I tried to convince myself it was true. It *was* true.

"Of course she's awesome, her sister is back." Tessa looked over at me. "She's not allowed to discuss it—ongoing investigation," she added quietly. I could tell she loved being my official spokesperson, and I was happy to let her have the job. She ran her fingers through her curls. "God, is there anything to drink at this thing?"

As if a switch had been thrown, Miles pulled his arm from my shoulder and put a finger up to his lips, whispering, "Shhh-hhhh, come with me, my pretties." He led us through an arched doorway and down a flight of stairs into a cozy den with leather couches, a massive flat-screen TV, and a pool table. He pulled a couple of beers from a small fridge under the bar. "Liam's dad and his girlfriend are upstairs, but they're cool. Just don't put any cold drinks down on the pool table—leaves a mark."

He popped the cap off a bottle and handed it to me. "For the girl who needs it most." He grinned. He offered beers to Tessa and Idina as well. I took a long swallow and let the cold bubbles travel down my throat. I didn't love the taste of beer, but there was something about this one that felt right: I liked holding it, the shape of the bottle, and being in Liam's perfect house with my friends. It felt normal, for the first time in a long time.

We found ourselves on a big leather couch talking to Miles and a few other guys from school. Some people asked, at first, about Sarah, or said things like "That's so crazy!" but then, as Mom had predicted, the conversation moved on quickly: who was trying to get with Kelly, the freak-out that Idina had in chemistry when she got a 60 percent on her exam.

I scanned the crowded room for Max's little brother, Gabe, knowing that seeing him would be the strangest part of the night, but it looked like he hadn't shown up, and I was happy for it. The beer made the muscles in my neck relax and I felt warm, safe.

I stood up to head to the bathroom and was surprised to feel my legs loose and wobbly, as if I had played tennis for hours. I'd never had a whole beer before, and this one tasted strong. Under the dim light in the bathroom, I could see my cheeks were pink, my eyes glassy. No one had noticed my haircut, not even Tessa.

I washed my hands and the water came out really hot, almost scalding. I tried to remember everything I'd said. Had I answered with the right words? Was I acting the way I was supposed to? Everyone seemed okay with what I had told them about Sarah, but now I wasn't so sure. My brain felt foggy, unreliable, like it had after Sarah disappeared and Mom gave me those pills to help me sleep and I couldn't trust my own memory. There was a knock on the door. "I'll be right out," I said. I looked at myself one last time.

When I came out, I practically crashed into the chest of a guy standing right by the door. "Sorry," I mumbled, not even looking up. A hand grabbed my arm and I spun around, alarmed, until I saw who it was: Daniel, a senior who worked on the school paper and yearbook staff with us. He was tall and cute, and had probably not actually spoken to me in the two years I'd been on the paper.

"Nico," he said, looking down at me. A little smile crossed his face and I noticed he had a dimple on one side. "I didn't know you were friends with Liam."

"I'm not, really, I mean—" I fumbled for something to say. "My friend Tessa is friends with him. And I guess I am too." I sounded like an idiot.

Daniel didn't seem to really be paying attention to my garbled answer. "I heard about your sister, I had no idea—you never talked about it," Daniel went on. "That's crazy."

I just nodded, not pointing out that I never talked about it because I'd never talked to him before. He had gone to a different middle school and probably didn't connect me with Sarah by the time we all got to high school. I tried to think of a response, something witty and light, but I was suddenly jostled from behind as a guy pushed past me into the bathroom, holding a hand over his mouth. The door slammed and we could hear retching inside. "That doesn't sound good," Daniel joked. He put his hand on the small of my back and guided me away from the door.

"So how is she, your sister? She okay?" He took a swig from his beer bottle and leaned against the wall. It all felt so casual, I almost blurted out a reply.

"Yeah, she is okay, she's doing good." I tried to give the same answer I'd been giving everyone all night. But something about the way Daniel was looking at me made me want to tell him more, to reveal something to him. To impress him.

He leaned down close to my face, as if to hear me better, and I could see the dark stubble on his cheeks. He reached down to touch my necklace, taking the wings delicately in his fingers and turning them over. "What happened to her anyhow?" I could feel his breath on my cheek.

"I don't know," I said, my mind still feeling a little foggy. "I mean, we don't really know yet. . . ." I wanted him to lean in closer,

I wanted to keep him interested. I looked over to the couch and saw Tessa staring at me, her eyebrows up like a question.

"Listen"—he took another sip from his bottle and slid his hand to my waist—"I just wanted to say if you need someone to talk to, like, anytime, let me know." I looked into his eyes—a deep chocolaty brown. "And if you ever need to skip a yearbook meeting, no worries, I've got you covered, okay?"

I swallowed hard. "Thanks, I . . ."

Miles suddenly appeared in front of us, holding out another beer. "I'm good." I started to wave him away, but he took my palm and pressed the cold bottle into it.

"Drink, and be merry," he said, trying to do a regal bow and almost falling down. "This girl has had a tough week," he said to Daniel.

Daniel just nodded, as if willing him to leave us alone. Miles got the message and went back to the girls on the couch.

"Cheers." Daniel clinked his bottle against mine. I put the cold bottle to my lips and took a long, deep swallow. It would feel good to drink it, to go deeper into that place, the place where it was easy to forget. But I didn't want to say—or do—the wrong thing. Not tonight. Not here.

When I brought the bottle down, Daniel was studying my face. "Nico, Nico, Nico." He shook his head with a slight smile.

I had no idea what he meant and I didn't know how to answer him, so I just stood there, nodding and looking stupid. I didn't do a lot of flirting, and didn't know how to start now. The only guy who had shown any real interest in me before was Max's little brother, Gabe, and I could never go there. No.

Daniel leaned against the wall as if he was just getting comfortable. He was about to say something else when I heard a voice from the other side of the room: "Hey, D, you in or what?"

I looked over and saw one of the senior guys holding up a pool cue. Another voice called, "Stop talking to that sophomore!" and the guys all laughed as they set up the pool table for a new game. I felt the blush on my cheeks creep down my neck and chest, making me blotchy with embarrassment.

"Yeah, I'm in," Daniel called over his shoulder, keeping his eyes on mine. "See you at school, Nico, 'kay?" I liked how my name sounded from his lips.

"Okay, yeah. Great," I said, too eagerly, as he walked away from me. My words hung in the air between us, playing over in my head and sounding worse each time. *Okay, yeah. Great.* Ugh.

I went back to the couch and squeezed in next to Tessa. "Daniel Simpson: so hot," she whispered. "What did he want?" She nodded toward the pool table, where Daniel now prowled, holding a cue low over the green felt like he knew exactly what he was doing.

"Nothing, just asking about Sarah." I took a drink of the beer in my hand, though I knew I shouldn't. I willed myself not to drink any more, just to hold the bottle like a prop so no one would try to give me another one. Get yourself together. *Nico, Nico, Nico.*

I tried to rejoin the conversation around me, but I couldn't help replaying what Daniel had said in my mind. My eyes kept going to the pool table, watching him, even as he finished his turn and joked with his friends—all of them tall and older, seniors like him. I felt my phone vibrate in my pocket and quickly slid it out. For some stupid reason, I thought it might be from Daniel. But it was from Mom: *Having a good time?* followed by a smiley emoji. I pictured her and Dad sitting there, worrying, waiting to see if I was okay. Suddenly, that sick feeling washed over me again and I was floating out of the room, the noise around me turning into a blurred hum. Tessa and Idina went on talking, laughing. Their voices cut through my head like a hot knife. I closed my eyes, but saw Sarah, that burned circle on her back. Who did that to her? Why?

I told Tessa I was ready to go.

"It's like ten," she scoffed. "Seriously?" Idina had gotten up and crossed the room to show some kids from school something on her phone. I saw Tessa eye the group with envy. "We just got here."

"I'm super tired. My parents don't mind getting me, you can stay," I told her. I almost wanted Mom to come, to give her something to do, to let her feel like she was saving me.

"Don't be wack, of course I'm going with you." She pulled out her phone and sent a message to her mom. "She'll be here in fifteen. Let's see who's upstairs, quick." She pulled me behind her, with a wave to our friends; I looked back down the stairs, but couldn't catch Daniel's eye at the pool table before we were out of sight. *See you at school*, wasn't that what he'd said?

I dumped the half-drunk beer bottle in a bin as we circled the upstairs and met Liam's dad in the kitchen. He seemed crazy tan for this time of year, and too fit to be a dad. Then he introduced his girlfriend, who didn't look much older than we were. "She's in law school right now," he proudly announced, squeezing her waist. Watching them, I could still feel the weight of Daniel's hand on my back, what that was like, to be claimed by someone. They were both drinking glasses of red wine and seemed not to care too much what any of Liam's friends were doing. I was happy that he didn't notice who I was—no recognition of being "that girl's sister," no questions.

We finally saw Liam on our way out and he grabbed Tessa in a hug, lifting her off the ground. "Where have you been—did you just get here?"

"We're leaving!" She giggled as he put her down.

"Hey." He clapped me on the shoulder, like I was one of his

buddies. "How's it going?"

"Okay," I started to say, then I realized he didn't really care, he wasn't even looking at me. He seemed super drunk already.

"Don't go!" he said to Tessa, holding her hand as we went to the door.

Tessa's cheeks burned red but I could tell she loved it. "My mom's already here," she said. "Sorry we didn't get to really hang."

Liam put on a fake pouty face, long blond bangs flopping over his forehead. He really was kind of adorable, I thought, as he watched us climb into the car from the doorway.

"Who's that?" Tessa's mom asked.

"That's Liam! Oh my God, Mom!" Tessa yelled.

"Oh, so that's Liam," she murmured. "Cute."

The whole ride home, Tessa only wanted to know if she had done it right—hanging out and being cool with the best friend, playing hard to get with Liam when he actually noticed her. "I don't want to jinx anything, but I think he really wanted you to stay," I reassured her.

"Right? He seems to be totally over Kelly. But still, have to wait a week at least," she pointed out. When we pulled up outside my house, it was still before eleven.

"Thanks for getting me to go and everything." I leaned into Tessa and hugged her.

"I'm just psyched you're back, I missed you! Call me tomorrow, 'kay?"

"Tessa, leave her alone, would you?" Tessa's mom joked.

I laughed and thanked her mom for the ride and went into the house. Mom and Dad were in the den. I could hear the TV on.

"Home so soon?" Mom asked. She pushed her reading glasses up on her head and closed her book. Dad was watching some sports coverage.

"Where's Sarah?" I asked quickly.

"She came down and had a little dinner, then back up to bed. She seems okay though," Mom said. "Did you have fun?"

"Yeah, it was good." I leaned in the doorway, not willing to sit down and let them get a good look at me, even though I was feeling pretty normal already—the effects of the beer had almost worn off. "You were right, people were really cool about . . . everything." I remembered Daniel's face, so close to mine.

Mom smiled.

"I'm going to bed," I said as Dad's eyes went back to the screen. On my way upstairs, I thought about the car ride home. Tessa and her mom never mentioned Sarah again; they had already moved on to other things: Liam, the party. And Mom and Dad, would they have mentioned her if I hadn't? I stood outside her silent door in the dark hallway, thinking about her inside. The room wasn't empty.

Sarah was in there. My sister.

I had gone out, to a senior party, just like a regular fifteen-year-old. I had been in Liam's huge house, seen how he lived with his father and that "girlfriend." That was normal for them. This was normal for us. Maybe we were slipping into being just another family again—maybe a regular life wasn't that far off for us.

CHAPTER 16

THE NEXT DAY, I sat at the breakfast table and tried to pretend that everything was routine, that we were just like any other family of four, and things were going so well in our house, it was easy to do. Mom was at the stove frying up a second batch of bacon and Dad was leafing through the paper. The new coffee machine that Mom bought, just for Sarah, was bubbling away on the counter. It could have been any Sunday morning in any home. Sarah, in her new pink pajamas, knees pulled up to her chest, barely looked up from the comics section. "Nico, you want to hear your horoscope?" she asked.

"Um, okay."

She scanned the paper in front of her, then looked up at me, a worried expression on her face. "I can't remember your birthday, your sign."

At that moment a memory came to me—Sarah, pushing my

tiny clay sculptures off my dressing table onto the floor, breaking the cat—the tiny whiskers, so hard to get right, scattered into the rug, impossible to find. *It's not my fault. Your room is a mess. Aren't Virgos supposed to be neat freaks? God, Nico. Clean up this crap.*

"I'm a Virgo," I said quietly.

"Oh, right," she said. She read a few lines about how I was going to need to focus on my work for the next few days—actually true, as I hadn't cracked a textbook since Sarah had come home, and I had school the next day. The prospect of facing everyone—my friends and teachers—made me push away my plate of eggs and toast, half eaten.

"I'm gonna jump in the shower," Sarah announced, standing and stretching. She brought her plate and coffee cup over to the sink. "Thanks," she said, giving Mom a quick embrace.

Once Sarah left the kitchen, Mom turned to Dad. "Did you see that?"

Dad put down the paper. "See what?"

"It's nothing, just that—Sarah brought her plate over without being asked, and gave me a hug." Mom stood there with the spatula in her hand and she and Dad exchanged a look of pure gratitude.

Dad smiled and shook his head. "She's grown up a lot."

The doorbell rang and, for an instant, we all held our breath. Detectives? Then I remembered, probably at the same time Mom and Dad did: Paula. She wouldn't leave yesterday without a commitment from Sarah to go running in the morning, "We'll do the high school track, Sarah," she'd said, "like we used to." But they hadn't agreed on a time, Sarah had never said yes.

Mom shot Dad a look. "Nico, will you tell Paula that Sarah's not up for a run—and we have family plans today," Mom said.

I let out a sigh and went to the door. Paula was dressed in running clothes, complete with ponytail under her baseball cap. "Where's Sarah?" She looked past me and into the house. The way she said Sarah's name gave me shivers. It was almost sarcastic, or like she was angry.

"She's not up for it," I explained.

"Okay." Paula nodded and met my eyes. Then she motioned for me to step outside on the porch and I did, pulling the door shut behind me. "Why don't you walk with me for a while. There's something I want to talk to you about."

What do you think you're doing, Nico, talking to my friend about me behind my back—did you think I wouldn't find out?

"I can't, we're doing something."

"Oh really." Paula tilted her head to the side, looking thoughtful. "Family time," she murmured. "Well, tell Sarah that we're heading back up to school today." I noted her use of the word *we*. "But I'll try to swing by next time I'm down."

"Yeah, okay." I turned to go back into the house, watching through the window as Paula crossed the street. She paused on the other side and looked up at the windows for a moment before she got into her car.

Mom came up behind me, wiping her hands with a dish towel. "The film Sarah wants to see starts in an hour and a half, okay?"

We had planned to take it easy today—spend time as a family before I headed back to school tomorrow and Dad went back to work. Sarah had a whole slew of doctors' appointments Monday that Mom had to take her to, and I knew she was stressed about them.

"I dunno about the movie," I said. "I've got homework, but you guys go." I took the stairs two at a time. Something Paula had said was still echoing in my head—no, not what she said, how she said it. *Family time.* As if we weren't a real family, as if we were just playing a game. I didn't want Mom to see my face.

I rounded the corner and ran into Sarah in the dark hallway coming from the bathroom and startled. My instinct was still to cower, to wait for the shove, the slap.

Nico, clumsy Nico, always falling and getting hurt.

"Oh, Nico, sorry!" She put a hand on my arm and I jerked back. "I didn't mean to scare you," she said sincerely. "Who was at the door?"

I paused and held my breath. The word *nobody* was on my lips. "Paula. She thought you might want to go running."

"Oh, right," Sarah said. She had probably forgotten that Paula even asked her yesterday. "Did she leave already?"

I nodded. "I told her you weren't up for it. . . ." I waited for her to say something.

You have to get cardio every day, that's what you don't understand, Nico. You're going to be blubber your whole life if you don't start working out.

Sarah rubbed her wet hair with a towel. "You okay with seeing this dumb movie? I know it's for kids, but looks kinda cute, right?"

"I can't, I've got piles of homework. School tomorrow." I backed into my room, but she followed me.

"What do you have? Anything I can help with?"

"It's advanced algebra, and I have midterms next week, so . . ." Sarah had never been good at math.

"Let me have a look." She moved to my desk and she picked up the algebra II book.

"Really, I've got it," I said quickly, taking the book from her hands.

"I'll get dressed and grab the chair from my room so we can sit at your desk," she said, dismissing my protests.

When Mom came up to get us for the movie, we were already halfway done with the assignment, Sarah carefully explaining each step of the complicated equations. It felt strange to sit so closely to her, to have her take the pencil from my hand without grabbing, shoving. *Uh, Nico, you are stupid, beyond stupid.*

She smelled like my shampoo and soap and lotion.

"You understand this stuff?" Mom leaned over my scratch pad of work, marveling. "Sarah?"

"I guess I just remember it." She shrugged. "But we're going to miss the movie I think, right, Nico? A couple more pages to get through and then she'll totally have this."

Mom stood behind us, her mouth slightly open in shock. Her daughter, asking to do math homework instead of seeing a movie. Sarah helping Nico with homework.

"Okay, that's fine, we'll see it another time," Mom said as she moved to the door. I saw her eyes water up before she turned to go.

By afternoon, I had not only finished my math, I was ready for the midterm—something about how Sarah explained the equations made it just click into place. She wasn't as helpful on the social studies. "Maps are just not my thing," she admitted. But it was still nice to have someone else there while I answered questions about ancient India and China.

"You girls have been working all day," Dad pointed out. "I think we should at least rent a movie and order a pizza—what do you say?"

"Or we could rent a pizza and order a movie," Sarah joked, doing an impression of Groucho Marx. I burst out laughing, I'd never seen her do anything like that before, so light and funny—not taking herself seriously.

Mom and Dad exchanged a look that I couldn't read, somewhere between amusement and bewilderment. "Let's do whatever it takes to get a pizza and movie happening in this house." Mom laughed.

I stuffed my books and notebooks into my backpack and hung it up while Sarah went downstairs to pick out pizza toppings. I took her chair back into her room and tucked it under the desk. Something under the desk at the back was blocking the chair. I leaned down and saw a black nylon bag tucked partway behind the drawers. I could hear voices from downstairs, Dad on the phone placing the pizza order. I kneeled down, listening for a moment before I reached under the desk and pulled at the bag. It was a small duffel I recognized as Sarah's. She had used it for PE clothes and her cheer uniform. What was it doing here, hidden behind her desk? She always kept it in her closet.

I slid the bag over the carpet; it seemed almost empty. I held my breath as I unzipped it. Inside was a hooded sweatshirt, rolled around a pair of black leggings and a shirt from Sarah's closet— old stuff, nothing from our recent shopping trip. The dirty pink flip-flops Sarah had been wearing when we got her in Florida were under that.

Why was she keeping these things hidden? I went to slide it back under the desk, when I noticed the outline of something in the front pocket. I almost didn't want to see what was there, but I unzipped it and reached inside. There was a business card with a hair elastic wrapped around it. *Carmen Rosa, Department of Children's Welfare and Services*, it read, with an address and phone number in Florida. I tried to remember if we had met a Carmen at the shelter. Behind the card were three twenty-dollar bills, carefully folded, and two slips of paper. As I unfolded the paper I felt my hands start to shake. They were blank checks, Mom and Dad's checks with our name and address on them.

A getaway bag. That's what this was. But why would Sarah need to run? She was home now. Safe. With us, her family. Wasn't she?

"Nico, if you want some say in the movie, you better get down here," Dad called. I startled, sticking the money and the checks into the elastic behind the card, and shoving it all back into the little pocket. I slid the bag where I had found it and pushed the chair in.

When I got downstairs, everyone was in the den. Dad held a glass filled with Scotch and ice in one hand and scrolled through movie options with the remote in the other. Sarah scooted over on the couch and patted the cushion next to her. I went over and sat down. Where would Mom sit? Usually it was just the three of us, Mom on one side of the big soft couch, Dad on the other and me in the middle. Now I was in Mom's usual spot, Sarah was in mine. It felt good to lean on the arm of the couch, to tuck a pillow behind me and cozy in. Mom came in with a tray of drinks and popcorn and placed it on the coffee table. Without a moment's hesitation she pulled the overstuffed armchair closer to the couch on Dad's side.

"What's the decision?" Mom asked, looking over the movie titles for something she recognized. "How about that one set in India, it's supposed to be really beautiful."

"Mom," I said curtly. "No one in that movie is under eighty years old. Please."

Sarah laughed, but agreed to just about anything as we went through the options, saying, "Oh yeah, that sounds good." It was strange to see, through her eyes, all the movie titles of the past four years—the big releases and the bombs—that she had missed. The huge teen blockbuster that she had never heard of, the dark romantic comedy that had won all the awards. She was open to anything.

When the pizza came, I watched in the darkened den as she took a slice of pepperoni, her eyes glued to the screen. *That's a bunch of leftover pig parts, you know, and so is bacon,* Sarah used to say. *Gross. They put the snout and the tail and everything in there. Of course Nico eats it, she'll eat anything. So disgusting.*

Sarah grabbed a blanket from the back of the couch and spread it over her own lap and mine, keeping her eyes on the screen as she thoughtfully tucked it down around me. My mind went to the bag under her desk upstairs, to the money and checks. I tried to picture Sarah packing them, folding the checks, sneaking them from the checkbook. But I couldn't connect those hidden things, those stolen things, to this girl sitting beside me—my sister.

SARAH

I NEVER SAW HIM again after that, after the burns. And she said, "Things are gonna change around here." And she meant it too. Things did change. First she put a special lotion on my back where he burned me. Those round dots got better in two or three days and I could even sleep on my back again after a week, with no bandages.

When it was a little bit better, she put me into the tub and washed me all over, telling me she was so sorry he had ever touched me but she was washing it off now. "It's like it never happened, okay? This soap is magic and washes away bad men like him." I believed her.

My hair hadn't been washed in a long, long time and I had sores on my head so she had to put on some special shampoo and comb it out. That hurt almost worse than the burns. I felt like big chunks of my head were coming off.

"Let's do this in front of the TV," she said, and let me wrap up in her robe. It was white and fluffy and sizes too big for me, like a huge marshmallow. I sat on the floor while she sat on the couch with the special comb and we watched an old movie as she worked on my hair. It hurt, but I liked being out of the room and watching a movie about a funny little man with a bushy mustache, even if it was in black and white.

CHAPTER 17

MONDAY I WENT BACK to school. The first day was no joke, with the expected stares and whispers, a required visit to the counselor in the morning to check in.

"Nico, have a seat." Dr. Weir welcomed me into her office. I glanced at the inspirational posters she had on the wall. One showed a picture of a juicy hamburger and asked, "Are you hungry to learn?" Another had an image of a ballerina on a stage and the words: "If you can DREAM it, you can DO it!" I stared at those words while Dr. Weir slid into the chair and paged through a file on her desk.

After we talked for a few minutes about Sarah and what had been going on for the past week, Dr. Weir said it seemed like I was handling things remarkably well and that made me feel pretty good. "If you need to talk about anything—anything at all, please know my door is always open and I'm here for you." She quickly signed the form that would allow me back into class and handed it to me.

I got up to go, grabbing my book bag and slinging it over my shoulder, but I stood in the doorway for a moment.

"Is there something else, Nico?"

I nodded, feeling tears well up in my eyes. I had not cried once since Sarah had been back, but now I felt like a wall was coming down, like I was finally ready to tell someone everything. Dr. Weir motioned for me to sit again and handed me a box of tissues. She waited quietly while tears streamed down my face.

I had spent a lot of hours in Dr. Weir's office. I used to see her once a week, a regular thing—my parents wanted me to have someone to talk to. After a few months of weekly meetings, you get comfortable with a person. I had cried in this office so many times, mostly about my parents—about Mom and how sad she was. About how it ate me up inside to see her suffer and feel powerless to help her. About how hard I had to work to be perfect, perfect, perfect and not ever give them any reason to worry. How I had to be different from Sarah, so different in every way.

I was totally honest about all of that. But I couldn't tell Dr. Weir everything. I never told her that, after years of cruelty from my sister, I sort of secretly liked being the only child. That I didn't really miss Sarah. I had never told anyone that. I almost couldn't think it, I knew how wrong it was. Like the thoughts I was having now. I just shook my head.

"Nico, it's okay to crack, it's okay to cry, you don't have to be perfect. We've talked about this before. No one expects you to be the perfect daughter, the perfect student. You can have feelings."

I nodded, hearing the familiar words. We had been talking about this, working on it, for ages. But if Dr. Weir or my parents knew just how far from perfect I really was . . .

"Tell me what's bothering you," Dr. Weir went on. "Talk to me."

"It's just that Sarah is really different now. I mean *really* different, like a different person, and sometimes I catch myself thinking stuff like . . ." The tears started again. I was too scared to say the words out loud.

"It's okay, you can tell me," Dr. Weir encouraged. "You start thinking what?" Her face stayed calm. "Let me ask you something. Did you think you would ever see Sarah again?"

"No." I heard my voice crack. "I thought she was dead."

"We all thought that, sadly," Dr. Weir said. "So, having Sarah back is like having someone come back from the dead. When you are pretty sure you're never, ever going to see someone again, and they return, that's a lot for your mind and your heart to handle, isn't it?"

I nodded.

"When you have to deal with someone being dead, gone forever, that's a grieving process that can't be undone overnight. And you almost don't want to believe they're alive, because you don't want to be hurt again."

I thought about all the dead blond girls my parents had seen. All the bodies, all the false leads.

"Getting used to having Sarah around is going to take time, that's all. You also can't expect that she'll be the same girl you used to know. It could take some time for *her* to readjust to being with her family. It's understandable that there will be some bumps along the way."

When I left Dr. Weir's office, I went straight into the girls' bathroom and threw cold water on my face. I covered my warm cheeks with the paper towels and never looked into the mirror, too afraid that I would see Sarah's old face there, looking back at me.

At lunch, friends we hadn't seen Saturday night crowded around our table and peppered me with questions. I was able to dismiss any speculation by explaining that Sarah had amnesia and by telling them I wasn't allowed to talk about it, since it was an ongoing case. Without any horror stories to pass around, talk eventually dried up and returned to what I had missed the week before. Until Gabe came up and tapped my shoulder.

"Nico, can I talk to you a sec?" Max's younger brother looked anxious.

I grabbed my tray from the table and followed him outside, dumping my trash along the way. Gabe looked like Max, but the junior version—he was smaller and wore his hair longer, as shaggy as our private school would allow, with a braided leather choker around his neck like a surfer. For about a minute, our freshman year, I think he wanted us to be the mini of Sarah and Max, and he started hanging out with my group whenever he could. At a school dance, he lingered in my peripheral vision, trying to sidle up to me and make conversation. It took Tessa discreetly telling him it was never going to happen for him to back off.

"Something's up with Max and Paula," Gabe said quickly. "Like, I think they're breaking up."

"Why?"

Gabe leaned against the wall outside the cafeteria. "I heard them fighting all weekend. Talking about Sarah. Mucho drama."

I thought back to how Paula had been at our house with Max— so possessive. Clinging to him. But Max hadn't been that way with her. When Sarah had disappeared, he was in love with her. And now it looked like he still was. Part of me was elated, knowing that Sarah would be thrilled with the news that her boyfriend might be hers again. But a little part of me, deep down, was bummed. Of course, Sarah got her way. Again. Without even trying. Paula had to be devastated.

I noticed that Gabe was the only one who didn't have questions about Sarah—Max must have told him everything.

When I got home after school, anxious to tell Sarah the gossip, she was upstairs. She had been at doctors' appointments all day and was taking a nap after the MRI they had done. I could hear Mom pacing in her office, getting records sent where they needed to go, from the shelter in Florida and over to the police. She needed X-rays from our pediatrician, but it sounded like they didn't have them.

When she came out and saw that I was home from school, she pushed her reading glasses up on her head. She hadn't checked with me to be sure Tessa's mom was driving us home and didn't even ask how my first day back was. "Oh, Nico, I'm so glad you're here. Tell me I'm not going crazy: Sarah never had a fracture in her arm when she was little, did she?"

"No," I answered quickly—that had been me. The time I fell down the stairs, Sarah standing at the top, looking down at me, a smirk on her face. An "accident," just another accident. "Why?"

She shook her head. "I don't know, they think the break in her arm might have happened earlier, like ten years ago or more, from how it's healed. But I was sure that couldn't be right. She's never broken a bone, from what I remember. But maybe a fracture, I mean unnoticed . . . from cheerleading, gymnastics, or something?"

I shrugged. I really couldn't remember.

"Well, someone broke her arm." Mom raised her voice, holding up a pile of papers. "You should see the things that have happened to her, it's not just the burns. What they did . . ." I could tell from Mom's face that she was talking about sex.

"Why does it matter?" I felt the words come out of my mouth and instantly regretted them.

"What is that supposed to mean?" Mom stood in front of me, her eyes narrowed.

"Nothing," I mumbled, heading for the stairs.

"Nico, stop. I want you to explain to me what that meant, right now."

I heard a small sound and looked up to the top of the stairs as a shadow moved there—Sarah, standing in the dark hallway, listening to every word.

"I just meant that I don't know why this stuff matters—if she hurt her arm before or last year, who cares?"

"We are building a case against whoever did these things to your sister," Mom pointed out. "And I want everything accounted for, every single thing they did. When this report"—she shook the papers in her hands—"when it goes to the police and the detectives, I want them to know about every burn, every broken bone, every time they raped her." She stopped there and met my eyes, looking daggers at me. As if what had happened to Sarah was somehow my fault.

"Okay," I said. "I get it. Maybe she did hurt her arm before—I remember her having a sling, from something—gymnastics."

Suddenly Mom's face changed with realization. "You know what, I remember that too—maybe it will be in the photo album, or Dad might remember. He has a better memory of these things."

I wanted to ask her what the MRI showed about her brain damage, if they had an explanation for how she had changed so much, but Mom was already digging open the storage closet, pulling down old photo albums. And I was glad not to have asked when I saw, as I went up the stairs, Sarah's door quietly close behind her.

CHAPTER 18

WE STARTED TO SLOWLY ease into a pattern of days as a family. I went to school, Mom stayed home with Sarah, and Dad went to work. I started to do my usual schedule again, with after-school stuff like tennis and the yearbook—everything but working at the help line. I had gotten a super-nice email from Marcia telling me to take a couple of weeks off to spend time with my family. "We welcome you with open arms as soon as you're ready to come back, and look forward to meeting your sister," she had written.

Sarah's schedule was pretty full. She had doctors' appointments during the day, mostly with a psychiatrist in the city—a two-hour round trip—but they seemed unhelpful for much other than her transitioning back into our lives.

"She still can't remember anything, not one thing—not how they got her to Florida or how many people it was or even if they were male or female or both," I heard Mom tell Dad one evening.

The detectives hadn't been back, but I knew that Sarah's doctors were obligated to share their reports with the police. Any detail might be the clue that would allow them to track down her abductor or abductors.

Mom's biggest fear was that whoever had taken Sarah let her go but might be holding other girls. Or what if they were running a ring of underage prostitutes, releasing them when they got too old to be interesting to clients? "They may have just replaced her with another girl, which means some other family out there is suffering like we were," Mom said. Her crusade continued, looking for answers and trying to right the wrongs. It was as if she had been doing it so long, she couldn't stop, even now that Sarah was finally home.

Part of me wished she would just let it go, so we could all move on. Sarah was back, our family was together, and I didn't want to question where she had been or what had happened to her anymore. But it was hard for any of us to let go when we spent our days constantly reminding Sarah of things from the past: stuff she had done, what she had liked or disliked. It was all simple things, like her favorite foods, actors and singers she liked. Once we told her, she seemed to remember. "Right, I saw all of those vampire movies already," she'd say, nodding. But I could never tell if it was true or if she just wanted us to believe that she remembered.

And nights—not every night, but a couple of times a week—she would wake with screaming night terrors. Mom usually went in to her and was able to calm her down quickly, but the whole house was awake until it was over, every time, her voice cutting through the dark: "LET ME OUT, STOP IT, STOP IT."

When I got home most days after tennis or yearbook, she and Mom were in the kitchen fixing dinner. Sarah often sat with me and helped with my homework, her calm, simple way of explaining things a welcome relief from Mom's shrill complaints that the teachers gave us too much work (covering for the fact that she was just as confused as I was about the math and science). Somehow, Sarah had a firm grasp on the subjects, and what was expected. "Next I bet you're going to have plate tectonics," she said, paging through my science textbook. And she was right. The teacher jumped ahead two chapters, just as Sarah had predicted.

"You should really be a teacher," I told her one night, and Sarah shook her head.

"Me?" she asked, the southern lilt returning, just for an instant. "I like to help you, but that's because you're my sister. I could not handle a whole classroom of kids." I liked the way she said *sister*. My sister. She pulled out the GED prep book Mom had picked up for her, and we studied together.

I had told everyone about Max and Paula, how it looked like

they might not be an item anymore, and I could tell from Mom's face that she was pleased, but she would never admit it. "Well, I'm sure it was something going on before, and not Sarah's fault," she said.

Sarah was harder to read; I had thought she would be thrilled with the possibility that Max could be hers again, but instead she seemed cautious. Max had planned to return on the following weekend and wanted some time with her—alone. The prospect of Sarah being out of the house with anyone but family was terrifying for all of us and became the main topic of conversation when Dr. Levine, the counselor from the center, returned on Wednesday night.

"Again, if Sarah feels ready for it, she probably is," Dr. Levine counseled. This applied to a visit from Gram as well, who was anxious to see Sarah even though her declining health made it almost impossible for her to travel. She had plans to come in the next week or two to see her oldest grandchild and stay with us for a few days.

That night, when I finished brushing my teeth, Sarah called me into her room. She was sitting on the bed, still reading *Rebecca*, only halfway through now. "Can you tell me . . ." She bit her lower lip and smiled a little. "God, this is so embarrassing!"

I sat on the bed and waited for her to go on.

"It's just . . . about Max, how I was with him, what we did

together," Sarah started to say. "I don't remember any of it, and I'm just worried. I don't want to disappoint him, he's gone through a lot, right?"

She didn't know—couldn't know—how much.

"It's just weird to go on a date with someone you haven't been with in four years," Sarah went on.

I nodded, thinking back over their relationship. What could I tell her? "You guys ran away once, to a cabin," I said. But Sarah cut me off.

"Yes, we went to his parents' cabin, up in the mountains and stayed overnight, right? That was why they thought I had maybe run away again, when I went missing. They thought I did it again."

The way Sarah explained it, I knew she had gotten that information not from her memory but from some newspaper story about her case. She couldn't know—wouldn't remember—how much that one night had changed all our lives. Even though it was four years ago, the memories were still so clear. Mom and Dad were frantic. When it got to be around two in the morning and Sarah hadn't come home, wasn't picking up her phone, they called the police. Then Mom called the local hospitals, giving Sarah's description, but they didn't have any patients who matched. Of course they didn't. I already knew that.

Because I knew exactly where she was. That time.

Sarah was with Max, at his family's cabin up north. A two-hour drive away. She wasn't in a hospital, she hadn't been in an accident, abducted, raped, left for dead somewhere. She was with her boyfriend.

Finally, after waiting up for hours, I couldn't take it anymore. My parents were in agony. So I told. Mostly because it wasn't fair for Mom to think her precious daughter had been hurt, or was lying in a morgue somewhere, but part of me also wanted Sarah to get in trouble.

Instead of being relieved when I told them the truth, my parents just seemed angrier. Angry at me for not telling sooner, and angry at Sarah for making them worry. They sent me to bed in tears, sick and sobbing, unsure if I had done the right thing or made the biggest mistake of my life. I was only eleven, but I knew one thing for sure: Sarah would make me pay. She always did.

After that, I saw my parents second-guessing themselves at every turn, questioning every decision. Even with me. I told Mom I didn't feel like going to tennis practice one day after school—Sarah had "accidentally" closed my hand in the bathroom door and my nails had turned black on two fingers and my hand hurt. Mom let me stay home, but it prompted a whole in-depth conversation after dinner with both Mom and Dad about whether they were pushing me too hard, and did I really want to take tennis two times a week, because if I didn't, that was fine with them. They were fine with everything; they just wanted me to know.

Even with all their concessions, everything they did, it wasn't enough. At the end of the summer, she disappeared again. Of course, the first person questioned that time was Max.

"The cops came down pretty hard on Max," I told her now. "And Paula too—the detectives thought they had something to do with your disappearance."

"Did they?" Sarah asked innocently. She met my eyes and I realized that she really had no idea.

I shook my head. "No," I said honestly. Max had been their number one suspect. They searched his parents' house, the cabin, even his car. Mom spent hours with the cops, trying to convince them he couldn't have done it. He would never do that. He loved her.

"Max would never do anything to hurt you, I know that," I said quickly.

"And Paula?" Sarah met my eyes for a moment. "What about Paula?"

I took a deep breath before answering. "You and Paula had some problems. . . ." I remembered the article from two years ago, the one that reopened Sarah's case. The journalist had really exposed the issues between the girls at school—the fierce competitiveness, the arguments—that stuff was all documented on social media, even though Paula had tried to delete some of it. They investigated the phone call that Sarah had received on the day of her disappearance and tried to interview Paula. She wouldn't talk, but that didn't stop the reporter from speculating.

I had heard later that the article made it hard for Paula to apply to college, that anyone could look up her name and find her connection to the case. The specter of Sarah's disappearance haunted both Paula and Max, casting a shadow of doubt on everything they tried to do. Was it any wonder they had found each other, had become a couple in the wake of that?

Sarah and I sat there awkwardly for a moment, neither of us speaking. I tried to think of what else I could tell her, to set her mind at ease.

"Max might want to see . . ." I pointed to my left hip. "Where you put the tattoo, of his initials. That little M and V."

Sarah looked down and touched her own left hip gingerly. "I gave *myself* the tattoo?" she finally said. "Why?"

"It was when Mom and Dad said you couldn't see him anymore, they told you he was too old. And Paula said you were dating him just to hurt her. You wanted to prove something." I paused, remembering. Sarah, coming out of the shower, wrapping a towel around herself. She knew I had seen the tattoo.

Now he's mine, forever. If you tell anyone about this, she said, *I swear*

*to God you will be so sorry. I'll kill you, I mean it, Nico. I will seriously kill
you.*

"I saw it by accident. You told me that you did it with a pin and
ink. I think they're still in your top drawer." I glanced over at her
white desk, my eyes traveling down to where I'd found the duffel
bag. Was it still there?

"Max has your initials, too—same place—in case you don't
remember that. But I think the whole thing was your idea." I gave a
weak smile and looked at her, but she just nodded, slowly, as if taking it all in. I stood up and turned to go.

"Nico," Sarah said, stopping me. "Thank you." Tears welled in
her eyes.

I shrugged, leaning against the door for a second. "What are sisters for, right?"

She nodded. "Right." And she met my eyes for an instant.

I pulled the door behind me, almost closed but not quite, the way
Sarah liked it now, and stepped into the dark hallway.

SARAH

SHE HAD TO PART my hair very carefully and comb it into braids to hide the red part on my scalp. I watched her hands in the mirror as they moved, quick and effortless. "I used to cut hair," she explained. "Still could if I wanted."

There was writing on her wrist, a name, but it was in cursive so I couldn't read it. "That's for my angel," she told me. "I don't believe much in tattoos, but I had to get this one. Had his name put on me so he's always with me. Hurt like a bitch, too, but it was worth it, every second."

When she was happy with my hair, it was time to clean the house. She kept talking about this person coming over, and how important they were—a Very Special Visitor, she said. When the person got there, I wasn't supposed to talk about *him*, or any of that stuff that had happened before.

We had to clean and clean everything, and then one day she came home with a new bedspread for me, with Disney princesses all over it. Pink and white and fluffy and perfect, it was the most beautiful thing I had ever seen. I knew the bedspread was just for show, just for the Very Special Visitor, and she didn't get it for me because she loved me or even cared about me, but it didn't matter. I kept it until I was seventeen, through all the moves and different houses and apartments and trailers where we lived, until it was no more than a bunch of rags and stuffing—that's how much I loved it.

CHAPTER 19

THE WEEKEND VISIT WITH Max didn't go as well as we had all hoped. Mom and Dad wanted Sarah to slip back into her old life: Max, school, friends, everything. But Max and her friends had moved on; they were all in college now. Max was a man, not a teenager. And the Sarah who came back to us was not the Sarah they remembered, not the one who Max had fallen in love with.

We all stayed up, of course, waiting for Sarah to get home that night. But she was home early, before ten. I was in my room, but when I heard his car outside I came downstairs. Sarah looked pale as she closed the door behind her.

"How'd it go?" I asked. I meant to say something more casual— *How was dinner?* But really what I wanted to know was: Are you two back together? Can you just pick up where you left off and be that golden couple again? I was dying to know if Max had really broken up with Paula and if he had done it for Sarah.

From Sarah's tense expression, I could already tell the answer was no. But she put on a smile for Mom and Dad as they came in from the den. They stood silently waiting, but Sarah wasn't talking, so we all just stood there awkwardly.

"How was that new restaurant?" Mom asked, her smile strained. "Dad and I have been thinking of trying it." She wanted this so much, wanted it for Sarah, for all of us.

"It was good, kinda expensive, but nice." She nodded. Everyone was silent for a moment or two, hoping she would go on. "Well, you didn't have to wait up," she finally said, then she stopped herself. When she lifted her head again, her cheeks were streaked with tears. "I'm sorry, you guys, I don't think he likes me anymore—" Her voice caught in her throat. "Maybe I'm just too different now."

Dad opened his mouth, then closed it. "I'll go get her something to drink," he said, turning to the kitchen. Mom and I pulled Sarah to the couch where we could sit on either side of her.

"It's okay, Sarah, it's okay." Mom pushed her hair back from her face. I saw the makeup she had so carefully applied just hours before, eyeliner and mascara, clumping under her eyes now, smears of green and black. I'd never seen my sister break down like this. Mom hadn't either. Even when Sarah was super angry and threw a tantrum, it didn't usually include tears. It was heart-wrenching to watch her thin shoulders shake with each sob; she was so broken already.

"Did something happen?" Mom asked, rubbing her back.

Sarah took the tissue I offered her and blew her nose, shaking her head. "No, nothing like that. He's super sweet, he's so nice."

Dad came back in with a seltzer for Sarah and put it on the table, but Mom waved him away. He stood looking down at us for a moment.

"Maybe some tea would be good," Mom finally suggested, giving him something to do.

As soon as Dad left the room, Sarah went on quietly. "It's just so clear that he doesn't find me attractive anymore. He didn't try to kiss me."

"That doesn't mean anything!" Mom protested. "He could just be taking things slow. Give it time."

Sarah looked over at me, her eyes red rimmed and raw looking. She grabbed my hand. "Nico, you know what I mean, right? When you can just tell a guy doesn't want you?"

I nodded, remembering Daniel's hand on my back at the party, his hungry smile. Did he want me? I almost had to shake my head to clear the memory.

"I think maybe I've changed too much." She looked down at my hand in hers and squeezed hard.

"No, it's not your fault," Mom said softly. "It might take a little while to click again. People change, that's all."

But Sarah shook her head, and I had a sad feeling she was right.

She wasn't that same girl anymore, and Max couldn't pretend not to be disappointed.

When she was calm enough and we had all had a cup of chamomile tea, I led Sarah upstairs. She sat on the edge of the tub in her new outfit. "Can you help me get this crap off my face?"

I took out the bottle of makeup remover and a few cotton balls. I tipped the bottle onto the cotton and slowly, gently wiped it over her eyes and cheeks, taking the smears of color away. I studied her face while her eyes were closed, how her lashes brushed her cheeks, the small freckles that now dotted her nose, the acne scars.

"Done," I told her, tossing the cotton balls into the can under the sink. I stood to go, but she pulled me back.

"Stay," she asked. So I sat on the closed lid of the toilet while she splashed water on her face, then brushed her teeth. She looked at herself with toothpaste suds still on her lips. "You know, I spent like two hours getting ready for tonight. I shaved. Everything." She shot me a look and I got what she meant. "What a waste."

I had to laugh a little. It was such a drag, putting in the time for someone who didn't appreciate it. I had been spending an extra fifteen minutes every morning getting ready for school, just in case I saw Daniel. So far, if I did the math, I had wasted over two hours making myself look good for him and had only seen him twice since the party.

"You know what?" She spat angrily into the sink. "Now I'm getting a little bit mad. Who does he think he is? Like he's so awesome? Maybe I don't like *him* anymore."

I nodded. "Yeah, he's not all that," I agreed. But picturing Max's handsome face in my mind, I had a hard time convincing myself. He was pretty hot. "I think you could do better, really. I mean, he's your high school boyfriend, right? Maybe you're over that."

Sarah dried her face and looked at herself closely. "Maybe I am," she said. She tipped her chin up and looked at herself from the side in the mirror. "Maybe I am."

The next morning at breakfast, Mom couldn't help herself. She brought up Max, and the possibility of giving him another chance.

"We'll see," Sarah said quietly, looking down into her yogurt bowl. "I doubt he's going to call me, and I'm *not* calling him."

"Why not?" Mom asked.

I let out a laugh. "You guys didn't even want her dating Max before, remember? Now you're bummed that they're not deeply in love."

"Nico," Mom said sharply, "that's not true. We always liked Max."

I exchanged a look with Sarah across the table. "I just hope he doesn't feel like he waited around for me or anything," she said.

"He wasn't waiting, he was with Paula," I mumbled. I wanted Mom to stop pushing for this. Why couldn't she let it go?

"Okay, Nico, I've had enough. Are you trying to be hurtful?" Mom asked.

I pushed my chair back and brought my bowl over to the sink without answering her. Why did anyone think it would be easy for Sarah to just slip back into her old life? For any of us to do that? I didn't want the old Sarah back, even if Max and my parents did.

Gram finally pulled it together enough to visit us that next week, and I couldn't wait to see her. It had been almost a year, and while I knew she had been sick, it was still a shock to see her coming off the plane at the airport in a wheelchair.

"I'm fine, I've got it," she said in a wavering voice as she stood from the wheelchair at the baggage claim, using a cane. Overnight, she had become an old woman. I hardly recognized her.

As if reading my thoughts, Gram murmured, "Getting old is a terrible thing."

"Maybe you should sit until your bags come," Mom offered, but Gram shot her an icy look.

Gram took Sarah's face into her hands and looked up at her, getting as close as she could, squinting behind her thick glasses. "Now, they said you looked different, but I don't think so. You're still my little Sarah, aren't you?"

Gram asked me about school as Mom searched the baggage carousel for her suitcase. "Her grades are really good," Sarah jumped in. "She's doing awesome."

I glowed under her praise. "I admit, I'm not in love with the advanced algebra," I added. "But Sarah's been helping me some with my homework, so at least I sort of understand it." I trailed off, looking over to Sarah to see how she would react to my crediting her, but she wasn't looking at me. She was watching a guy sitting behind us in a chair near the baggage claim.

I followed her gaze and saw him tapping a pack of cigarettes against his palm. His eyes were on Sarah as he pulled open a plastic tab on the box and slid a cigarette out. He tipped it into his lips with a quick motion and cupped the end, lighting it with a small plastic lighter. He put the lighter back into his jacket pocket and gave Sarah a little half smile. Sarah seemed in a trance, watching him. The smell of burning paper, of sulfur, met my nose.

He shook one cigarette from the pack and extended it to Sarah, wordlessly. She stood numb, unblinking.

"You can't smoke in here, young man," Gram huffed, turning slightly away from him. "My goodness."

The guy leaned back into his chair and pulled a hard drag from his cigarette, keeping his eyes on Sarah's. I noticed a dark tattoo that wound around his wrist and underneath his jacket sleeve.

"Found it!" Mom said in a singsong voice, rolling Gram's dark pink suitcase up alongside us. She seemed not to notice the guy with the cigarette. "Let's go—your dad should be right out here with the car." She walked to the door and I turned to follow, but Sarah didn't move, as if she was locked into place.

Mom took a few steps before she realized it, looking back at her. "Sarah?" she said quietly, pulling her from her daze.

Her face softened as she looked at Mom. She smiled and moved quickly, taking Gram by the elbow, helping her out to our car at the curb. When the glass doors closed behind us, I turned back and saw that the guy was still there, blowing smoke—watching Sarah.

After we got Gram all set up in the guest room and she had some time to rest, she kept insisting on taking us out for ice cream. This was something she used to do when Sarah and I were little—on every visit, we would get into whatever car she had rented (usually something bright and convertible), and she would take us to the dairy farm about half an hour away. I realized later that she was probably giving my parents a break; we would be gone for a couple of hours. And it also gave us time to visit with Gram on our own, just the three of us.

I loved when Gram came because Sarah was always on her best behavior. Gram would not allow any "nonsense," as she called it, so Sarah knew not to act like such a raging bitch when she was around. I also felt that, unlike my parents, Gram saw Sarah for what she was, and took my side a lot. She would shoot Sarah a look sometimes that said *I see through your bullshit*, and that would usually shut Sarah up in a way I'd never seen from anyone else. The drive out to the farm meant listening to the radio with the top down, the wind in our hair. I never even argued with Sarah for the front seat or control of the stations—just let her have it, so we could avoid any fights.

"Yogurt? I don't want *yogurt*, frozen or otherwise," Gram complained when Dad explained that the old dairy farm had closed last year and offered to drive us to the fro-yo place instead. We finally settled on an old-fashioned ice-cream and coffee shop downtown. Dad parked and Sarah and I both had to help Gram climb out, pulling her up from the seat. When I put my hand on her arm, I felt her skin, warm and soft, under my palm.

The place was filled with twentysomething hipster types drinking cappuccinos and lattes. But Gram, unintimidated, strode up to the counter and placed our order loudly. "Two pistachio nut ice creams in bowls, and one mint chip in a sugar cone," she recited.

When the ice creams came, I took my cone and carried Gram's

bowl to a table. Sarah looked down at the other pistachio, confused. "Is this for me? I thought it was for you." She glanced at Dad.

Gram stopped stock-still on her way to the table and turned to look at Sarah. "It's your favorite, dear, mine too. That's what we always get." Sarah reluctantly picked up the bowl of green ice cream and sat at the table. While we ate, Gram filled us in on her latest medical problems and test results. It was all slightly hard to understand—her calcium levels were up, her bone density was down, she had a pinched nerve and a bad hip. Dad asked questions and nodded, sipping his coffee while Sarah and I exchanged a look over the table. She rolled her eyes as Gram went on complaining and I hid my smile behind my ice cream. It was nice not being the only grandchild, having all the focus on me, as it had been for the past four years. Gram didn't ask anything sensitive. It was as if we all just slipped back into our old roles. Sarah left her pistachio nut almost untouched on the table, but no one else really seemed to notice.

When we got home, Gram asked that we get her settled out on the back porch "just for a spell," even though the evening spring air was still nippy. "Sarah, come out here and visit with me," Gram said. "Close that door behind you."

Mom started dinner and Dad mixed them both drinks while Sarah and Gram chatted outside. I could hear their muted voices from the kitchen. "Nico, can you set the table? Let's put Gram on the end here, so she can get in and out of the chair with her cane."

I walked around the table, carefully laying out cloth napkins and silverware and trying to catch what was being discussed outside, but I could only hear murmurs, not much more. Eventually, Mom flicked on the porch light and opened the door. "Dinner in ten minutes, you two."

In a few moments, Sarah led Gram back inside, holding her elbow as before. When they came to the table, I noticed that Gram's eyes were watery and red. Sarah's mascara had smeared under her lower lashes.

"You've got some . . ." I motioned under my eyes.

Sarah ran her index finger under her lower lids, asking, "Better?"

I nodded.

When we all sat down, Gram asked that we take hands. "Let us pray, and give thanks that our Sarah, my grandbaby, is finally back with us," she said, her eyes filling again as she bowed her head.

CHAPTER 20

DAYS OF SARAH BEING back turned into weeks, and soon the cool spring air started to change over to summer heat. Dad spent a weekend getting the pool ready and trimming back the shrubs in the yard while Sarah and I went shopping for new swimsuits at the mall with Tessa.

"Are they still really bad?" Sarah said, turning her back to us in a string bikini. Mom had been taking her to the dermatologist for laser treatments on her burns, but they were still there.

Tessa's eyes narrowed. "I can barely see anything, I would never notice," she said, looking to me to chime in.

"Much better," I lied, looking at the pink and peeling spots. They had said full healing could take months or years, and even then the scars would still be visible, just not as bad as before.

When we grabbed lunch at the food court, Sarah seemed more relaxed. Gone were the days when she was so nervous in public—scared of crowded places, of anyone recognizing her. We hit up the makeup samples at Sephora after lunch, and Sarah expertly applied a cat's-eye with dark liner to Tessa's lids, making her look like an old-fashioned movie star. As I snapped a few photos with my phone, I saw what anyone else would see: three teen girls, having fun together on a Saturday afternoon.

Tessa leaned in to hug Sarah. "I'm buying this," she said, palming the liner. "But can you come over, like, every morning and do my eyes?"

"Of course!" Sarah smiled.

Later, Tessa would tell me how much she loved my sister. "She is awesome, you're so lucky. I wish I had a sister." She had never known Sarah before, and I was thankful that she had forgotten—or chosen to forget—the portrait I'd painted of my sister before she'd returned.

As the weather warmed and the days lengthened, everything got easier, just like Dr. Levine had predicted. The detectives and reporters stopped calling. It seemed that the investigation into Sarah's reappearance was following the same course as her disappearance— slowly falling away from people's minds.

And Dr. Levine was good for something else too—a bit of marriage counseling for Mom and Dad. They started a new Friday "date night," at her recommendation, leaving me and Sarah to do our own thing. We usually ordered a pizza and rented a movie, nothing special—sometimes Tessa came over, too, but mostly it was just me and Sarah. The only thing that was off-limits was horror movies—anything where girls were being chased or in peril. They seemed to set off Sarah's nightmares, which still came about once a week or so, but could happen all night if she watched anything scary before bed.

Even though it wasn't a big deal, I found myself looking forward to our nights on our own. I began planning our pizza order, discussing movies with Sarah days before. Once I came home on a Friday afternoon to find a rack of chocolate chip cookies cooling on the counter. "You know, for movie night," Sarah said, scrubbing the cookie pan in the sink. I knew that she looked forward to it too.

I decided I was ready to go back to work at the teen help line, and went one spring evening after the time change—it felt weird to be there while the sun was still up, filling the call center room after a long winter of dark afternoons. It was like a new place. That wasn't the only thing that was different: as soon as I walked in the door, Marcia came over to pull me into a hug, a warm embrace that felt real, and she held me for a few moments. "I want you to meet someone, Nico," she said softly. She led me to the seat where I usually took calls, but it was already taken by a petite girl with short dark hair.

"This is Shivani. She's your trainee." Marcia smiled.

"Hi, I'm Nico." I shook the girl's hand and added, "I love your bangs," noting the thick straight cut she was pulling off—it was striking.

Shivani blushed. "I know who you are." She smiled. "You're, like, famous."

I swallowed, caught off guard. Famous for what? Then I realized: Sarah. Marcia cut in, "Shivani specifically asked to train with you, and I think it's a great idea."

I didn't know what to say to either comment. The fact that Marcia thought I was ready—and good enough—to train someone else at the help line, or that Shivani considered me a mentor. I pulled over a chair, sitting close to her, and found a splitter for our headphones. "We'll take some calls together to start, sound good?"

I surprised myself by how quickly I slid into the role, the older student, the trainer to the trainee. It had only been a year ago that I was in Shivani's place—how much had changed over the past few months. As if by some other divine act of good fortune, the calls we took together were really routine: a girl who was thinking of running away, another whose parents' divorce was sending her into a spiral of depression. Nothing that Marcia had to step in for. As I gave advice and spoke to each caller, I heard the calm confidence in my voice over the headphones—it surprised even me.

When it was time to wrap up for the night, we left together, stepping out into the cool spring night, our breath visible as we left the warmth of the lobby. "Nico, I just want to say thank you so much," Shivani said as she headed to her parents' car. "This means, like, everything to me."

I suspected the freshman girl would tell her friends at school that we were friends—that we volunteered together—as if it was a badge of honor and prestige. She would likely brag about it, but that didn't bother me. I had noticed since Sarah's return that some people, especially kids at school, were interested in me in a new way, intrigued. For a few, that faded once Sarah had been home a couple of weeks. But for others, it was as if I had been invisible before and now they saw me. One of them was Daniel.

Ever since the party at Liam's, he had been acting differently toward me at our yearbook meetings. For one thing, he actually knew my name. On days when we met after school, Wednesdays, I spent forever getting ready, trying on uniforms in the long mirror on the back of my door in the morning, trying to find one where the skirt fit just right, my navy cardigan snug over a white top. I would wash and blow out my long, blond hair and wear it down, instead of up in a ponytail or a loose bun like I usually did.

"Must be Wednesday," Tessa teased, scooting in next to me in homeroom, taking in my carefully crafted appearance.

"Is it?" I would joke back, pretending to look at the calendar by the teacher's desk. Of course Tessa knew that I liked Daniel, but unlike the way I encouraged her crush on Liam, she was decidedly negative about my feelings. "He's got a different girlfriend every week," she pointed out. "Not a good sign. The best you can hope for is to be that girl—for one week. Really? You want that?"

The truth was that I didn't want that, I wanted more—something I couldn't even confess to Tessa or Sarah, that I could barely admit to myself. I watched Daniel closely, and yes, he did seem to date a different girl every weekend and flirt expertly, with just about everyone. But as far as I knew, he hadn't found anyone to ask to the senior prom yet. As the date approached, a fantasy grew in my mind. We would be working on the yearbook, scanning in photos, and he would lean over my shoulder, checking something on the computer screen. "This looks good, can you move this one a little to the left to make more space for the header?" and I would hold my breath, waiting for it, with his body so close to mine. For him to look in my eyes the way he had at the party. To see that hungry smile.

Sometimes he did. Especially if I stayed late, if we were a small group and ordered in something for dinner with Mr. Stillman, our art teacher, as the only chaperone. When he sat next to me at the long design table, teasing me about being the youngest person on the staff. "This one here is trouble," he would joke, putting his hand on my back. "She looks so innocent and pretty—if anyone is going to sneak a prank into the yearbook, it's Nico." I would blush and mumble something. But for all his flirting, he never actually made good on the imagined promise, the dream that he planted in my head at Liam's party, that maybe I was something special to him.

One rainy day, when we had PE inside, I heard the girls in the locker room talking about prom and someone mentioned Daniel. He did have a date, and had for weeks, a girl he had gone out with a few times. She was a sophomore, too, but dark haired, curvy—the polar opposite of me. I ducked into the bathroom and felt tears sting my eyes. How could I have been so stupid? It became clear to me, all in a rush, that Daniel had only noticed me in the first place because Sarah had returned. All the time I had been dreaming about him he had probably not thought about me once.

As the date of the prom approached, Mom and Dad were actually wondering if Sarah wanted to attend, since she had missed hers, but she laughed off the idea. "That's okay," she admitted. "I don't feel like I need prom pictures to round out my teenage experience." On one of our Friday nights, we had just watched an old '90s movie about a prom gone wrong, and I think Sarah was happy to have nothing to do with that nonsense.

There were all kinds of prom after parties, and Tessa managed to somehow get us invited to the one at Liam's house—her long-held fantasy of being together with him had not faded. "He's going to be a senior next year, and I'll be a junior—it's perfect," she explained to me and Sarah while we were getting ready.

Sarah nodded, standing behind her in the mirror and braiding Tessa's curly hair into a halo around her head. "A woman with a plan, I like it," she said. "And what about that guy you were into, Nico? Is he going to be there tonight?"

"Daniel." I shrugged, trying to act very nonchalant. Inside, I was nervous he would come to Liam's party, but this time with his date. I had to look perfect, just in case he noticed me. Maybe there was still a chance to make him wonder why he hadn't paid better attention. To show him he'd made a big mistake, he had asked the wrong sophomore to the prom.

"He's super hot, but kind of skeezy," Tessa added, pushing a stray curl off to the side of her face. "Nico can for sure do better than Daniel Simpson."

Sarah glanced over at me, trying to read my face. "I've always loved the name Daniel, and that story with the lion's den." She smiled.

"What lion's den?" Tessa asked.

Sarah was searching through her makeup bag absentmindedly. "You know, in the Bible story, Daniel, the lion's den—they put him in there, but the lions don't eat him because God protects . . ." She looked up suddenly at me and saw no sign of recognition on my face.

"Oh, I don't know the Bible at all. My family isn't very religious," Tessa admitted.

It was on the tip of my tongue to say that our family wasn't either, but I caught myself. Tessa leaned in to look at her hair in the mirror, turning to Sarah. "Will you do my eyes like you did at the mall?"

Sarah held up the tube of liquid liner.

"You should come to the party with us," I suddenly said to her. "Come and meet Daniel and Liam for yourself."

Sarah looked like she was actually considering it for a moment, then smiled and shook her head. "Too weird," she said. "Besides, I've actually got to study."

Tessa and I both groaned. She was taking her GED studies so seriously. Though I wouldn't admit it, I was actually super proud of her. So were Mom and Dad, who remembered all too well the Sarah from before—the girl who wouldn't crack a book unless she was threatened with all kinds of curfews and punishments.

When I got home from the party later and found Sarah sitting at the kitchen table with her GED book out, I slumped down next to her. "You didn't miss anything," I had to confess. "And my feet in these heels are killing me."

"Daniel?" Sarah asked, raising her eyebrows.

I shrugged, getting up to grab a drink from the fridge. "He showed up," I said. How much should I tell her? That he was drunk, that his date was a mess, with smeared lipstick staining both her mouth and his? The truth was, when he finally got there, I was already having fun talking to a guy in my grade from my tennis team, Kyle. And there was something else, something bigger and darker that loomed in my thoughts when I looked at Daniel now. A realization that made him repulsive to me.

"He's a senior anyhow, he's got a month left in this town and then he's gone," I reminded her. "I don't want that—can you imagine Mom and Dad? It would be like . . ." I shook my head. At the party, I'd had a horrible epiphany when Daniel walked through the door, his arm draped over the curvy brunette.

He was a senior, she was a sophomore.

It was Sarah and Max all over again. I had craved it, dreamed about it, wanted to follow in her footsteps, without even realizing it. How could I have been so naive? When I looked into the mirror, I saw the same face, the same figure Sarah had when she was fifteen, but I wasn't her, and I never would be.

"But I didn't go to prom with Max," Sarah said, and I watched her face as she figured it out on her own. "They wouldn't let me," she said, looking at me for confirmation.

"That was when you guys first ran away, to the cabin—you were so mad. It was like you had planned it for months, and then they didn't let you get your prize, to show him off."

Sarah nodded, as if remembering. "And the matching tattoos, they came after that, right?" She closed her book on the table. "There will be other Daniels, I promise you, Nico," she finally said. "When you're ready."

Before school let out for the summer, Sarah managed to ace her GED on the first try and also helped me win second place on my science fair project. There was even a picture of me, posing like a total dork holding my red ribbon, in the yearbook. I finished the year with an A-minus in math—a first for me.

Mom and Dad hadn't put together any special travel plans for the three months I would be off from school, unsure of what Sarah might like to do. But she was content to just lie by the pool most days with a pile of magazines and her sunglasses, or to join me and Mom at the club, where another weird side effect of her amnesia became apparent: she had completely lost her tennis game. She couldn't even seem to remember how to score, and her old tennis skirts hung loose off her hips. "Sarah, you have to move back to the baseline, this is doubles," I told her for the tenth time, but she would just smile and bounce to the other side of the court, letting

Mom and her tennis partner cream us again. And she didn't even seem to care—Sarah used to be so competitive, she would slam her racket down and storm off the court in a huff when things didn't go her way.

"Thirty–love is bad, right?" she asked, adjusting her visor.

"Yeah, it's bad, unless you're trying to let Mom win," I said.

After yet another humiliating loss, Sarah laughed it off in the locker room. "Face it, Nico, you took all the amazing hand-eye coordination, and I got none."

"You used to have it," I pointed out, then quickly caught myself. "Sorry, I . . ."

Sarah rubbed her neck with a towel and smiled. "I can barely hold up my racket at the end of that beatdown!" She grinned at Mom and her friend Erin as they came into the locker room.

"The winners have to buy the losers lunch again?" Mom joked, knowing full well that everything at the club went onto their account.

As soon as we ordered our salads and iced tea, a girl with short blond hair and dark sunglasses approached our table. "Hi, all," she said, twirling her racket.

It seemed to take Sarah a moment to remember who Paula was, maybe because of the sunglasses or because we hadn't seen her in weeks. "Oh, Paula!" She stood and moved to embrace her. "It's so good to see you."

Paula's smile was tight. "Saw you all out there on the court and I could hardly believe my eyes, Nico. You've gotten really good," she said.

Sarah spoke before Paula could criticize her. "And I know I'm the embarrassment of the Morris family," she joked, pulling out a chair for Paula and patting the seat.

"Not at all," Mom said quickly, reaching for Sarah's arm. "You'll get it back—you're just rusty."

Paula chimed in: "Everyone knows the Morris family can play tennis, right? It's in your genes." She paused, glancing at Sarah. "I'm sure it will all come back to you."

No one at the table spoke for a moment, until Mom passed a menu over to Paula. "We've just ordered, if you'd like to join us." I could tell from her tone that she was just being polite.

Paula shook her head. "I can't stay," she said quickly. Then she looked over at me. "You know, Nico, I emailed you but I must have the wrong address or something."

"Yeah, I guess." I poked at my salad. I had gotten her emails.

"There's a club tournament coming up in a few weeks—you should really sign up for the under sixteen," Paula said, as if explaining her emails. But her notes hadn't been about tennis.

"Oh, Nico, you should," Sarah encouraged. "You would totally win. I'll come and watch—and try not to embarrass you."

"The sign-up sheet is almost full, so if you want in, you should do it pronto," Paula pointed out.

"Go do it, Nico," Mom said.

"I'll show you where you sign up." She swung her racket in her hands.

I swallowed hard. "I'll do it on our way out."

"By then it might be full." Paula smirked at me. "Come on, I'm going that way anyhow."

I stood, my legs feeling shaky below me.

"Good to see you all. Let's get a game going one of these days, okay?" Paula smiled as she led the way out of the dining room and into the front of the club.

When we reached the front room, Paula led me to the big dry-erase board, where players were signing up for the tournament. There was an older woman in front of us, putting her information down. We stood there awkwardly for a moment, before Paula spoke quietly.

"The happy family, out together," she started. "Where's Max? Aren't those two an item again?"

I shook my head. "They went on a date, or whatever, but . . ." I trailed off, feeling like I had said too much. It was clear that Paula and Max weren't on speaking terms. I wondered how hard the past few weeks had been for her. To all appearances, it looked like her former best friend had returned and stolen her boyfriend again. I didn't know how to convey that Sarah hadn't meant any harm, she didn't try to break them up. It had just happened. "It's not like they're dating," I added.

"Oh really," Paula said in a tense voice. She was registering the fact that Max had broken up with her—his girlfriend of two years—for nothing. Less than nothing. It had to hurt.

"You know, after Sarah went missing, the cops asked me a lot of questions. Max and me. But especially me. Do you know why?"

I tried to think back to the days right after Sarah disappeared. They were such a blur. "Because you called her that day?" I guessed.

"Because my fingerprints were on her bike. Do you remember that?"

I did remember. "Yeah, but you had borrowed it or something."

The old woman moved away and Paula picked up a marker, yanking the top off like she was angry. She handed the marker to me.

"That's what I told them, that I had used her bike, but I felt like they didn't believe me. For a long time, it seemed like they thought I had something to do with Sarah going missing, because we were fighting. Or that Max did. I was questioned twice, once with a lawyer, at the police station. Do you know what that's like?"

I had to shake my head. "I'm sure it sucked," I offered. I looked at the board, trying to figure out where to put my name on the bracket.

Paula let out a light laugh. "I had to take a lie detector test. And then that reporter with the huge article, making it look like Max and I were murderers. 'Sucked' doesn't quite cover it," she said. "To be honest, part of me was glad that Sarah was gone—I thought she had probably run away again, but left Max here this time. Maybe he was too small-town for her. I even thought that maybe you had helped her." She looked at me closely. "That's why I didn't tell the cops *everything* about that day. But they knew I was hiding something. My story just didn't check out."

I held the marker over the board, scared to even write my name. For a moment, I almost wrote *Sarah Morris*. Her name was a constant, running in the back of my mind, and had been for four years. With Paula standing next to me now, whispering into my ear, I was the one in danger of disappearing—didn't anyone see that?

Paula leaned in and whispered, "Do you know what I said when I called Sarah that day?"

I didn't answer her, just kept my eyes forward. *Nico*, I finally scrawled. *Nico Morris*.

"No one knows. No one but me. And Sarah." Her tone changed, her voice grew darker as she whispered. "I told her I was going to be waiting for her at the park. I was so angry at her, I could have killed her." Paula's whisper became a hiss. "But I didn't have to."

I focused on breathing, wondering what she was going to say next.

Paula looked around us, as if to make sure no one could hear what she was saying. "And now, Sarah is back. Someone kidnapped her, that's the story—isn't it? And took her to Florida?"

I knew it wasn't really a question from her sarcastic tone, so I focused on the board, slowly writing my contact info into the bracket for my age group.

"The thing is, Nico"—Paula leaned close to my ear—"as soon as I saw her, I knew. And you knew too, didn't you?"

I felt blood rushing into my head, a pulsing sound in my ears. "Knew what?"

Paula took the marker from my shaking hand and put the top back on. She carefully placed it at the bottom of the dry-erase board before answering.

"She's not Sarah."

I stopped breathing.

I felt as if the ground below me would swallow me up, like a big black hole was opening again, the hole Sarah left when she disappeared.

"So, who is that girl living in your house?"

SARAH

SHE SAID TO CALL her Ma, and so after that day, I did, when other people were around. I mostly called her by her first name when it was just us, though. And she called me by my name, the name my real mother had given me, even though I knew she hated it.

"You know what kind of name that is? A hippie name." But she didn't change it, she didn't ask to change it, and she could have, when she took me for good. Instead, she shortened it to a nickname.

First we had to be interviewed, though, by the Very Special Visitor. This was the lady who came to the house and asked me all kinds of questions. But Ma had told me just what to say to everything. And she dressed me so that you couldn't tell my arm had been broken or that I had burns on my back. And she braided my hair so you would never know that, at the age of five, I had cradle cap.

After the lady asked me lots of questions, she turned to Ma. "Do you think she's ready to start kindergarten in the fall?" And Ma nodded her head.

"Oh, she's a smart one, this girl, smarter than me. Show her that book you like so much, Liberty."

I ran to my room, all done up now and pretty with the new blanket on the bed and curtains and a pink rug. I pulled the illustrated Bible book from the shelf and brought it out to show it to the lady. I couldn't read, but I had every story memorized by the pictures. She seemed really interested so I told her every one. "My favorite," I said, "is this one where the man gets swallowed by the whale. Or this one, with the nice lions."

Both Ma and the lady laughed and the lady said, "Liberty, you are a true delight. How lucky you are to have her. We don't usually find a match right away for these foster kids, but I think we may have this time, I really do." And Ma nodded, smiling at me.

That night, there was ice cream—chocolate chip, my favorite— and Ma said, "You did good, kid. We're a good team, aren't we?" And after that we were. A team.

CHAPTER 21

THE THOUGHT HAD BEEN waiting just below the surface, in that realm where dreams from the night before swim, nagging at me, trying to tell me something. It had been there, but I hadn't wanted to think it, *really* think it. The truth.

Sarah.

She had been my worst enemy, my torturer. She made my life hell. She hurt me, with her words and with her hands. She made me hate myself, and I hated her.

Yes, I hated my own sister. Yes, I wished for her to die. And yes, my life got better when she disappeared. Paula's did too—at first. We both got what we always wanted. Even though it came at a price—a steep and terrible price.

Now Sarah was back, but she wasn't the same Sarah. She was the sister I always wanted, I always needed. She was kind, open, loving, to me, to Mom and Dad. I liked her—I loved her, even. I was not going to let Paula ruin this for me, for my family. No.

I heard the words of the school counselor coming out of my mouth. "If you think someone is dead, and they come back, it can take a while for you to get used to having them around again." I was talking fast as Paula cocked her head to the side, hand on her hip. "The school psychologist explained it to me, it's actually really normal to have doubts."

"Have you finished signing up?" A man stood impatiently behind us.

"Oh, yes, sorry." I moved out of the way, hoping he hadn't heard anything we'd been saying.

Paula grabbed my elbow and led me to the side of the front doors. "I've got to go. I have to get back." I tried to pull away from her.

"Back to what? That girl who claims she's Sarah? That stranger— Are your parents in on this too? Do you even know who she is?" Paula hissed.

"She's Sarah!" I spat, wrenching my arm free. I heard my own words, the lie I'd been telling myself for months, because I couldn't face the truth—what had really happened to my sister that day at the park. If Sarah was back, it had never happened. None of it.

I walked quickly away, imagining Paula behind me, but when I turned to look she was gone. I stood on the stairs that led down into the dining room and looked at my family, my mother and my sister, sitting so close together, their identical blond heads, Sarah's light brown roots just starting to show.

I thought about the night she had come home from her date with Max, how she had crumbled, broken. The screams of terror in the night. Looking at her, I couldn't bear the idea that someone would hurt this girl. That someone had burned her, tortured her, made her feel unloved, unworthy. But someone had done it.

My breath slowed as I watched them, laughing, Mom stirring sugar into her iced tea, Sarah ordering dessert from the waiter. She looked up and caught my eye, her face warm and open as she smiled and waved me over. I couldn't help but smile back.

Sarah had been home for months now, and everyone else thought it was her. Everyone knew it was her. Max, Uncle Phil, even Gram when she came to visit.

The problems between Sarah and Max were easily explained too. Sarah told me all about their last conversation: Max had confessed that he blamed himself. He was supposed to meet her on the day she disappeared. When she didn't show up, he assumed she had been pissed and left. He thought he would see her again. "I can't stop thinking about what would have happened if I had been there just fifteen, twenty minutes earlier, like I said I was going to be," he told her.

I hadn't known that, for all these years, he had been living with that guilt. And seeing how Sarah was now, the damage that had been done, he couldn't seem to get over it. Sarah told me he cried almost the entire time.

I tried to tell myself, as the long, hot days of summer wore on, that Paula would drop her craziness and leave us alone, as soon as she went back to the university. But anytime we were out—and especially at the club—I dreaded seeing her again, feared that she might say something shocking to my parents or to Sarah. But what she actually ended up doing was far, far worse.

SARAH

MA NEVER MADE ANY pretense that she wanted to be a mother or anything like that. He was the one who had wanted kids, and she couldn't have any. Or she didn't want to, after her first baby died, Billy, whose name she wore in a cursive tattoo on her inner wrist. So they got me out of foster care. I wondered what I was doing there—Had my real parents ditched me? Had I been adopted from birth, then put back into the system? My memories from before age four are just fragments: someone brushing my hair, someone yelling, a dark room. I don't even remember the place I was staying before Ma came and got me. When I asked her about my history, she didn't know much, or anything, really, about how long I had been there or what my story was. "I was *using* then, Libby," she always said. "You could have been dropped at my door by a family of clowns in full getup and I wouldn't remember it." I knew it was hard for her to talk about that time, so I only asked once or twice, then I let it drop.

After he was gone, she got clean. That took some doing, and a few relapses: nights of screaming fits, no food for days. She didn't feel like going back to her waitressing job. She decided she liked the checks. She liked not working. And to be honest, she did like me a little. Or she started to right around then. I think after she kicked him out, she wanted someone around. I watched the shows with her during the day and she started to take me with her, sometimes, when she went to the store. She would always light up when people would say "What a pretty little girl!" and "Don't you look just like your mom." With her hair a ratted, yellow blond, her teeth bluish from so many years of drugs, she loved the idea that she was seen as someone's mom, practically the Virgin Mary.

At night, she went out on her own and left me in the house, still locked in my room, so I wouldn't "get up to anything." But she always came home the next morning and never left me for more than a day. And after she got clean, even that stopped.

Before kindergarten started for me in the fall, we had another talk, a serious talk like we had before our Very Special Visitor. About what I could say at school and what I couldn't say. I wasn't allowed to ever, ever mention him. No one could see the marks on my back. If anyone asked about my arm, well—that happened before I came to live with Ma. We went over it lots and lots of times until I had it all memorized. We were a team, the two of us. Me and Ma. We had to keep our stories straight or they wouldn't let us stay together. "And you never know where they'll put you next," she warned me.

It was then, at age five, that I learned: The longer you tell yourself a lie, the more you believe it, until finally, it becomes your truth.

CHAPTER 22

I HAD ALMOST FORGOTTEN that I'd even signed up for the tennis tournament; I blocked it out of my mind along with everything else that had happened that day. But Sarah remembered. A couple days before the tournament she got busy picking out a winning outfit for me, and insisted that I take my racket to be restrung. She even picked out new laces for my tennis shoes—to match the skirt, of course.

"Looking good is half the battle," Sarah explained, trying a new visor on me at the sporting goods store while they worked on my racket. "High ponytail out the top—or maybe a braid?" She looked at me quizzically.

I laughed. "I'm going to be the best-dressed loser on the court."

"Don't even say that," Sarah scolded. "If you tell yourself you can't, then you're right—a teacher told me that once, and it's true."

I wondered who had told Sarah that.

"You have to believe in yourself, in your own self-worth. Remember when we were doing your math homework and you would always say, 'Oh, I'm so bad at math' or 'I'm never going to get this'—but you did, didn't you? You got an A in math this year." She pulled off the pink visor and put on a bright turquoise one as I stood in front of her like a mannequin. She paused and met my eyes. "As much as I think you're going to win, you have to believe it yourself to make it happen." She put her hands on my shoulders and her face was serious as she added, "But not in this color, because it washes you out." She pulled the turquoise visor off and hung it back up, opting for the soft pink.

We went to the register and Sarah took out the credit card Mom and Dad had given her, paying without even glancing at the price tag. They wanted her to have some independence, a sense of herself as a nineteen-year-old, so they had opened a bank account for her and given her a credit card. I thought about those blank checks she had hidden in the duffel bag behind her desk and tried to convince myself there was a reason they were there. Maybe Mom and Dad had given them to her, for emergencies. Mom had also signed her up for driving lessons, but she hardly needed them. "You're a natural, like you've been doing this for years!" the instructor exclaimed. She could parallel park with one hand on the wheel like the valet guys at the club.

So far I hadn't seen her abuse the card, but she really enjoyed nice things—one remnant of the old Sarah. The best restaurants, clothes, makeup, shoes. But Mom and Dad seemed to want her to indulge and they never complained. She was making up for lost time, in their eyes, and deserved every comfort after what she had endured.

We went out to the parking lot and climbed into Dad's Mercedes, the car he didn't even let Mom drive, and Sarah skillfully backed out and navigated us home, chirping about tomorrow's match and how I needed to carbo-load at dinner. "I've got it!" She hit the steering wheel with her palms. "How about that Italian place that Mom loves so much?"

"Palermo's?"

"Yeah, let's do dinner there tonight—pasta, pasta, pasta. And bread—that's what you need."

"It's so fancy, and pricey," I protested.

She looked over at me, a small smile on her face. "How often does my little sister play a tennis tournament? Come on, I'll ask Mom when we get home."

And I knew there was no way Mom would deny Sarah anything she wanted.

I didn't realize until the next day, when we parked at the club, that my nerves weren't so much about the tournament but about running into Paula. I knew she had signed up in the older category, so seeing her was unavoidable. I had thought about pretending to be sick and skipping the whole thing, but Sarah was so crazy excited for me, I just couldn't let her down.

I checked the schedule as soon as we got in to see which court I'd be on, and scanned down the brackets for Paula's name, but I didn't see it listed anywhere. Maybe she had chickened out, or she was too embarrassed about the stupid things she had said and done to show up.

I walked out for my first match full of confidence—the relief at not having to see Paula washed over me and I felt invincible on the court. I cleaned up easily, winning 6–1, and hardly broke a sweat.

"I told you pasta was the thing!" Sarah grabbed me as soon as I stepped off the court and wrapped her arms around me. Mom and Dad looked on, smiling politely—I don't think any of us had grown used to how much Sarah hugged and touched us all now.

I went on to win in the afternoon as well, Sarah's eyes glued to the courts with an intensity that would rival a personal coach at Wimbledon. This match was closer, 6–4, but I still managed to pull it off and get myself into the semifinals the following weekend.

That night, as we celebrated at home, the dark cloud over my head began to lift. We didn't have to see Paula or deal with her ever again, I knew that now. She would be heading back up to the university soon, would go on with her life and leave us alone. Once she got over Max dumping her, she would forget all about Sarah, would stop sending me stupid, vague emails. We could all go on with our lives and put Sarah's years of disappearance behind us.

I told myself that, and I really believed it. Until Monday morning, when the doorbell rang. Dad was already at work, Mom was at the gym with her trainer. I was upstairs getting into my bikini, so Sarah opened the door. I heard voices as I came down, men's voices. I recognized Detective Donally as soon as I got to the foyer, wearing his full three-piece suit even in the blazing summer sun.

"Hey there." He looked over at me. "Just the girl we wanted to see."

"Our parents aren't here right now," Sarah said protectively.

"Do you know when they'll be home?" the detective asked.

"I'm not sure," Sarah answered fast. "Not until tonight." That wasn't true; Mom would be home within the hour.

"Okay then, we'll stop by later," Detective Donally said. He squinted his eyes at me, as if studying my face. "You girls have a nice day." Sarah closed and locked the door behind him, watching through the window as his unmarked Ford pulled out of our driveway.

"What did they want?" I asked her quietly, watching over her shoulder.

"He said they had some questions," Sarah started to say, "for you." She turned to me and I saw that her face had gone ashen white. "He said someone involved with the case had come forward with new information."

"Paula?" I asked, hearing my voice break on the syllables.

"He didn't say." Sarah reached over and took both of my hands in hers. "Why do you think it's Paula?"

The emails. They had started two years ago. It wasn't long after we had Azul over to the house, for her stupid psychic vision. So when I got an email from someone calling themselves "SarahsFriend," I didn't know who it could be, but I had my suspicions. The first message said: *I saw you.* That's all. Just three words.

Then, a week later, another message, from the same account, "SarahsFriend." Again, just two words, but this time: *I know.*

I saw you. I know.

I deleted them, fast, pretending it never happened. Weeks went by, and no new emails. Then another one showed up, asking: *Where is she?*

Then nothing for a while. *I'm going to tell.*

I realized it could only be one person: Azul. Blackmailing me, or trying to. Shaking me down for cash—she had already taken $250 from my parents for nothing. The way she said "There is someone who isn't telling you everything. . . ." Did she really have a vision, or was it just a hunch? She looked at me like she knew. Knew that I wasn't telling. And I never would. Maybe she wasn't such a bad psychic after all.

It didn't take me long to track her down. She worked part-time at some new age store one town over. I told my parents I would be late at school, working on the newspaper, and that Tessa's mom would drive us home. Instead, I hopped a downtown bus after school. It took one more transfer and a long walk in the slush to reach the Healthy Mind Emporium. By the time I got there, it was already growing dark, the winter sun dipping below the roofs of the gray buildings.

The door chimed with brass bells when I pulled it open, and I was hit in the face with a strong stink of incense. Maybe that's why Azul smelled so funny—she spent all day in this place, her clothes and skin soaking it in.

"I'd like to see Azul," I told the blond guy behind the counter.

"She's with a client. Do you have an appointment?" he asked.

"I'll wait." I walked around the shop, picking up different tarot decks and candles, looking at the prices as if I was really interested in them before putting them back down. Finally, an older lady came out from behind an Indian print curtain and paid the guy at the register. When the bells at the door chimed her exit, I heard him say, "Miss? You can go back to see Azul now."

I pushed through the curtain into a dark hallway and saw Azul sitting in a small room at a table. She looked different, and it took me a moment to realize she had a scarf tied over her head, covering her wild hair. She was shuffling a deck of oversized cards as I walked in. "Hi there." She looked up at me. "Are you here for a tarot card reading or a psychic reading?" She looked into my face as if she had never seen me before.

I swallowed hard. "You know why I'm here," I finally managed to say.

She stopped shuffling for a moment and studied me with her brows furrowed, then she suddenly laughed. "Oh, I get it. A psychic joke! I *should* know why you are here. Hmmm, I would guess tarot reading." She smiled innocently. "Am I right? Have a seat, sweetie."

I pulled out the chair opposite her and sat lightly, ready to jump up if I needed to escape. But the longer I looked at her, the more I realized she had no idea who I was.

"Have you had your cards read before?" she asked, cutting the deck.

"No." I shook my head. "I mean, no, I don't want a tarot reading. That's not why I'm here."

Azul put her hands on the table. "Psychic reading?" she questioned. "How old are you, anyhow? If you're not eighteen, a parent needs to be here with you."

"You came to my house," I reminded her. "About my sister."

Still, Azul's face was a blank.

"You said you'd had a dream about her, a vision. Then you did this reading, you held her stuffed bear. . . ."

"Oh right," she said vaguely, as if trying to place me. "Uh-huh, and was that helpful to you?" She picked up the cards again, absentmindedly shuffling. "Is this a follow-up session?"

"My sister has been missing for years. You said she was probably dead," I pointed out.

Azul raised her brows. "I don't think I would say that—I might have mentioned that you would not see her on this plane of existence anymore. What is your name again?" she asked.

"It's Nico Morris. My sister's name is Sarah. Sarah Morris."

"Right." She nodded. Then suddenly, recognition. "Oh, I remember. You all are over by MacArthur Park, right? That missing girl, blond girl. There was that big article about her in the paper."

The newspaper article. I realized all at once that the emails hadn't been from Azul. They couldn't have been. She had gotten her $250 and she was gone. She didn't care about us. She didn't even remember Sarah or me.

"Did you send me a letter or something?" I asked, just to be sure.

"No, sweetie." She tilted her head to the side. "If you paid for the visit, there would be no invoice mailed or anything. Unless you want one. Is that why you're here?"

I shook my head. "I have to go." I pushed the chair back hard, the wooden legs screeching on the floor. "This was a mistake."

"Well, you come back if you ever do want a tarot reading, okay?" she called after me as I raced through the curtain.

The guy at the counter said nothing to me as I pulled the door open, clanging the stupid brass bells against the wall. I ran down the now-icy sidewalks, skidding to the bus stop, where I waited under the cold bluish light for my bus to come. My cheeks burned red, not from the cold but from embarrassment. How stupid I had been! Of course it wasn't Azul. And suddenly, I felt sick, my school lunch rising up my throat. I threw up into the black-lined garbage pail next to the bus stop, knowing just one thing: If Azul hadn't sent those emails, someone else had. Someone who knew. Someone who saw.

Now I knew who that person was. Two years ago, when the article came out, Azul had obviously picked it up. Took my parents for suckers, and her plan worked. But Paula had been mentioned in the article too. A photo of her and Max together, smiling. And the questions started: Why was Sarah's best friend dating her boyfriend? Did she know something—did they both know something? The speculation. All eyes were on Paula. I remembered the fallout afterward. How colleges rejected her, how her friends even looked at her differently. Her parents separated, finally divorced. Instead of making her life better, Sarah's disappearance had made things worse, much worse. Max was the only one she could go to. And me. Then Sarah came back, and everything was about her, even Max. The fragile life Paula had built was crumbling again. She wanted someone to blame. But now she had gone further than vague emails; she had gone to the police.

"Nico?" Sarah asked again, yanking me from the dark memories, back into the situation we were facing. "Why do you think it's Paula?"

"Because, she . . ." I couldn't finish the sentence, couldn't tell her. "Because she knows," I burst out. I leaned into Sarah and cried on her shoulder while she gently patted my back, asking for no more details.

She pulled back from me and put her hands on my face, looking me straight in the eye. "Nico, we're going to fix this. Don't worry. We're a team, right? Me and you," she said, pulling me in and wrapping her arms around me. "We're a team."

SARAH

IT WAS JUST A game. That's what Ma said, like dress-up. Sometimes we pretend to be other people. The first time we played was when the Very Special Visitor came to the house. I answered her questions the way Ma said to, even if it wasn't totally the truth. But it wasn't lying because I was playing, pretending. Pretending to be someone else, a little girl who was happy, who hadn't been burned and broken. And it worked.

Later, it became more complicated. We had to move when I was in second grade because Ma had written some checks that the landlord tried to take to the bank too soon. "I told him to wait until Friday—now look what happened!" she screamed as she tossed our clothes into garbage bags that would have to work as luggage and hauled them out to her van.

When we went to the new place, an apartment with only one bedroom, Ma told me how to act, how to be, what to say. I was her sister's kid, she said. Her sister was dying of cancer, we were just collecting money to help take care of her. People gave and gave, sympathetic looks and dollar bills. "No checks," Ma said. "Cash."

Of course, Ma didn't even have a sister, but nobody had to know that. It was the Stranger Game. We were strangers, and could be anyone we wanted—anyone you wanted us to be.

"You're awfully good at this." Ma eyed me as we sat in the front of the van, counting the money in the coffee can she had given me to hold on the street corner. There was a Polaroid of a sick-looking woman taped to the front, and a note that said *Please Help My Mommy*. I was eight years old, and flipped through the bills, doing the math in my head. I handed the stack to Ma, announcing, "That's seventy-eight dollars, or about forty dollars an hour."

Ma took the wrinkled bills and straightened them on her lap, shaking her head. "You're almost too good at this, Libby."

Later, when I was in eighth grade, my math teacher, Ms. Lay, pulled me aside after class one day. She told me I had a special skill—an ability to do math problems, even complicated ones, in my head without scratch paper. "How long have you been able to do this?" she asked.

I looked at the clock—I was about to be late for PE. "I dunno." I remembered counting out bills for Ma, organizing our fake cancer collection into denominations, from the time I was six or seven years old. "Forever, I guess."

Ms. Lay wanted to talk to me after school, about something called the Mathletes. "It's a group of kids I've put together, my best students. We go to competitions, all around the state. I think you'd be perfect for it."

When I told her I'd think about it, she went ahead and got in touch with Ma directly. Ma was actually pretty proud of me, to my surprise. "Your math teacher says you're something special, some kind of genius or something," she told me when I came home. Ma was usually only interested in how things could make money for her, so a math competition in another town was not high on her list of things to do. But she said I could go, if Ms. Lay drove me.

So I went, in Ms. Lay's car with a couple of other kids, eighth graders. Her car was nice, a silver color on the outside and had AC inside—unlike Ma's old van. We quizzed one another on the ride there, throwing out hard equations. Even though I did pretty good in the car, I was nervous before the competition. I'd never been on a stage in my life, and here we were, face-to-face with another group of math kids, competing. Ms. Lay must have noticed, and she sat with me backstage.

"Libby, I need to tell you something." She took off her thick glasses as she spoke. "You aren't just good at math, you're the best, most promising student I've ever had." She gave me a weak smile, then leaned over and hugged me before I went on stage. "You can do this," she said quietly. "I believe in you." I carried the feeling of that hug, of her arms around me, onto the stage and into the competition.

The first few questions were tough, but then I got the hang of it and worked with my team, bringing in lots of points. We demolished them, winning a small silver cup and a certificate. Ms. Lay took us to a burger place on the way home where we celebrated. She dropped into step beside me as we walked back to the car. I was the only girl on the team. "I'm profoundly proud of you, Libby," she said. And I could tell from her eyes that she meant it. She was profoundly proud.

On the ride home, and for days after, I would repeat that sentence in my head, over and over again. Even after we had to move, suddenly—another eviction—and I went to a new school midyear, Ms. Lay stayed in touch, encouraging me to continue my studies, to push myself. I lost touch with her when I dropped out of high school a few years later. But sometimes, when Ma was yelling at me, or I just felt like a loser, I would close my eyes and let the memory of that day, of Ms. Lay's words wash over me. *I'm profoundly proud of you.* That feeling. I did something great, someone cared about me, believed in me. I made someone proud.

CHAPTER 23

SARAH WAS FAST, ORGANIZING everything in an order that I could follow, even though my mind was racing. "First, you're going to go upstairs, throw some water on your face. No crying," she cautioned. "Then change out of your swimsuit—when Mom gets here, we're not going to be home."

"We don't have a car," I pointed out. Dad had taken his to work, Mom had hers at the gym.

"Right." Sarah nodded, looking over at me. "Put on something you can walk in, hiking clothes."

Mom would never believe we had gone on a hike in this humid weather. But maybe a bike ride. "We can take the bikes," I said. Sarah's bike had never come back from the police, but she could take Mom's.

"Great idea—go, go." She motioned for me to go upstairs and she went out to open the garage. When I came down, changed, moments later, I heard the familiar *tick-tick-tick* as she led my ten-speed out of the garage. I looked out the window and saw her blond head, the white tennis shorts she wore over her swimsuit. Sarah taking her bike out of the garage. *Tick-tick-tick.* The sound of the garage closing.

"Nico?" she called to me, snapping me out of my memories. I pulled on my shoes and swallowed back the bile that was coming up my throat. "Just follow me, okay?" she said. "Don't ask questions, just follow."

We got on the bikes without a word and turned left from the driveway. After we rode in silence for a few moments, Sarah turned right, and I knew where she was taking us. And I knew why.

It was time for the truth.

MacArthur Park.

The last place Sarah was seen, where her bike was found.

But I didn't want to go there, I couldn't go there. I hadn't been inside the park in four years. I almost couldn't even look at it—when we drove by, I closed my eyes and held my breath. On Sarah's birthday, my parents made me go, but just to the entrance.

I saw you.

Paula's email flashed in my brain like a neon sign.

I saw you.

Of course she couldn't tell the cops, couldn't say she was there that day. She knew how that would look. She had called Sarah—threatened her. But she did go, she went there to confront Sarah, to hurt her, and instead she saw . . . what?

I kept pedaling toward the wrought iron fence ahead, the archway over the main entrance, the gates swung open. People were coming and going, sitting on the edge of the big fountain just inside the gates. Picnic blankets spread on the grass, toddlers in a playgroup chased bubbles. A group of campers in matching green T-shirts lined up for a hike as a counselor counted them. It could have been that day. Years had passed, but it was all the same.

Sarah stopped her bike and got off next to the big gate. She looked back at me, her sunglasses so dark I couldn't see her eyes. As I pulled my bike up alongside her, she said quietly, "Do what I do. Act normal, okay?"

I nodded, but she didn't even look over at me. She walked to a guy with a handcart. "Got any lemon pops today?" she asked brightly.

The guy slid open the lid and pulled out a frozen lemonade. "This do?"

"Two please, one for me and one for my sister," she said. I watched her slip a carefully folded twenty from her pocket into his hand. He made change and she pocketed only the bills, giving him back the coins as a tip. "Thanks."

We took the frozen pops and sat on a nearby bench. I felt sweat run down my back under my tank top. Sarah opened her frozen lemonade and ate it like nothing was wrong. After a few moments, I had to ask, "What are we going to do?"

Sarah let out a sigh. "Well, we're going to do what we need to do, right?"

I shook my head.

"Nico, eat your pop, you'll feel better." She let out a light laugh. "Listen, the detective has questions, we're going to give him answers. Okay?"

I peeled back the paper on the frozen lemonade and the first bite was so sour and good, it went straight to my brain, as if turning it on for the first time in a long while.

Sarah kept talking. "Paula told him some things, he needs answers to those specific things—whatever they are. Then it will be fine. You'll see."

"But what did she tell him?" I asked.

Sarah turned to me and balled up her wrapper. "I don't know— you tell me, Nico."

SARAH

I DIDN'T COME UP with a plan to take Sarah's place. And Ma didn't either. To be honest, I don't think either one of us had the smarts to come up with an idea like that. It just happened, by accident. We were at a Best Buy near Gainesville with a new credit card and a new ID for me. Of course, the fake ID, stolen with the card, had me listed at twenty-five and I was only sixteen, but places like Best Buy almost never ask for ID; if they do, they just glance at the photo to see that it matches the name on the card, and mine did.

Ma was busy looking at flat screens, pretending that we were outfitting our new house—her favorite version of the Stranger Game—when a salesperson came over to help. In the middle of explaining the latest technology, he turned to me. "You know who you look like—that girl who went missing from Pennsylvania, what was her name? Blond girl." He squinted at me suspiciously.

I just shook my head, having never heard about the case. "I don't know," I told him honestly, and I didn't. He seemed to let it drop, so we went on shopping. When we were done, it took a clerk with a flatbed cart to wheel all the stuff out to the van: new huge screen, a surround sound system, DVD player. The works. And the credit card had gone through no problem.

But as the guy was loading up Ma's van, two Gainesville police cars pulled into the lot and we knew it was trouble. "Ditch the cards," Ma whispered to me, so I opened my purse and tossed the credit card and ID under the car next to ours in one swift motion. A shame, as the fake ID had been a tough one to make and it looked pretty damn perfect.

"Evening, ladies." One officer approached us. Two other cops went into the store.

"Yes, can we help you?" Ma said, clutching her receipt tightly.

"Oh, it's not about your purchases here tonight—we just had a report that your daughter matched a missing person report from another state and we wanted to come and check it out."

"Who, Libby?" Ma laughed, looking over at me. "Well, she's not missing, I can tell you that!" She laughed a little too loudly—relieved that the cops were here for some nonsense and not the fact that we were basically stealing thousands of dollars of merch from the electronics store.

The cop took out a small black notebook and asked me a couple of questions, and I answered them—giving a fake last name, but not the one on the credit card. Where did I go to school? What was my birthday? He jotted down a few things in his notebook. He looked up at me, studying my face, then looking at a folded piece of paper he had in his hand. "Yeah, I can see the similarity"—he shook his head—"but you're not her," he said finally.

"Who are you looking for?" I asked. Ma shot me a look that said to shut my mouth and get into the car.

"This girl, she's about your age." He showed me the piece of paper. It was an image of a pretty blond girl, her name across the bottom and the words *Missing* and *Possible Kidnapping* stood out to me. I just glanced at it quickly before he folded the paper and put it back into his notebook.

"Hate to say it, but they should be looking for a body at this point," the cop said quietly. "She's been gone months, and, well, you know how these things go. Anyhow, sorry to have bothered you. Y'all have a good evening now."

He nodded at Ma and headed back to his cruiser. Ma handed the guy with the cart a five-dollar tip. "Thanks for your help—we're so excited to get all this set up at home!" she added cheerfully. I knew that we wouldn't be setting up anything, we would sell it, probably by tomorrow morning, at a discount price. Still, it would be a cash sale, and that money would be ours. We casually climbed into the van and pulled out of the lot, Ma watching for lights behind us.

"I was hoping to hit the liquor store on the way home, but now I don't know—we should just get on," she grumbled. I knew she was mad about the ID and the credit card, but there was always more where that came from.

CHAPTER 24

I CLOSED MY EYES and tried to block out the bright, hot morning sun, the sounds of the park around me. It could not have been more like that day if I had planned it. That had to be a sign. But a sign of what? "Okay," I finally said quietly—not so much to Sarah as to myself.

I stood up from the bench and Sarah followed my lead, pulling her bike over to the rack. I knew where her bike had been on that fateful day, and carefully moved us to the other side. I couldn't do that, let her lock the bike in the same spot.

Without speaking, I walked woodenly past the group of campers, third or fourth graders. They had been told, I was sure. *A girl went missing here, years ago, and they never found her. So walk in a line, no going off the path . . .*

Past the fountain, the oak tree with the plaque commemorating a long-ago battle that took place here, to the slope at the back of the park, where the trails began. I knew where the back trail was, the one that led up to the picnic area. It was shorter than the main trail by half a mile, but it was steep. Too steep for bikes. The goat trail, we had called it.

I stood at the bottom of the main trail, looking at the sign for a moment. Carved in wood:

CRYSTAL LAKE 0.5 MILES

PICNIC AREA 0.8 MILES

We started up the main trail, then needed to cut right. I surprised myself by remembering exactly where to go, like I was in a dream.

"This way." I moved through the brush at the side of the trail, stepping over a low wooden railing, where a path had been worn by feet and had no sign.

"Careful," I told Sarah, realizing she wouldn't know, "sometimes there's poison ivy here."

We started up in silence, the slope of the trail gaining as we went, so narrow you had to put one foot in front of the other. It grew so steep, the earth below us almost formed steps, carved into the hills. I stopped to catch my breath, wishing that we had brought water. The tart sweetness of the lemonade pop lingered in my mouth, making it feel dry and tacky. Sarah looked up at me, leaning on her knees and breathing hard.

"Almost there," I told her. Because she had never been here before.

More steep steps leveled out into a trail—still upward but not at such an acute angle. I was pushing through now, hearing Sarah's breath behind me as I went. I didn't want to get there, but then I did. I had been waiting such a long time. And now it was real.

This was no dream.

At the place where the goat trail reconnected with the main trail, it came out under a low oak tree, the branches hiding the way until you were practically on it, blocking the beautiful view of the lake, just below the cliffs. I stood there, leaves touching my face, until Sarah caught up. She said nothing, just stood beside me, breathing hard. I stepped out of the darkness of the goat trail and onto the wider main trail, where sunlight filtered down, the glittering lake off to one side.

"She came up this way, I knew she would, because she had her bike," I said. "She was meeting him at the picnic area. I locked my bike down at the rack, took the back way up, the goat trail, so I got here first."

Sarah lifted her sunglasses and wiped sweat from her face with the back of her hand.

"I thought she would be biking. But those boots. They had

slippery bottoms, no treads. They weren't good on the pedals. I had forgotten that. So she was walking up, and pushing her bike along."

Sarah looked up and down the trail, as if checking for other hikers, but we were alone here.

"I didn't mean to scare her. I just wanted to cut her off." I almost let out a laugh, remembering her face, the O of her mouth. At first, it was wonderful, the rush of adrenaline, the joy of catching Sarah, of being the one in control, standing above her on the trail. But then her anger.

Nico, what are you doing here, you stupid bitch!

"Mom and Dad said she had to take me, or she couldn't go. But she didn't. She left me, like I knew she would. She always did whatever she wanted." I moved my sneaker over the dusty trail, rolling a rock under my sole. I didn't want to say it out loud, what I knew deep down, about myself.

That I hated Sarah.

I hated my own sister. And she hated me.

Something inside me had snapped that day, when she stood over me with the sweater. I was done. I was tired of always tiptoeing around her. It was always about Sarah, what she wanted. No one ever thought about me.

"I knew when she got home, she was going to make me lie for her, say she took me along. Or say that she never went. And she would get away with it too, with my help—because she always got away with everything."

Sarah stood silently, just watching my face.

"She always got her way." I looked out over the lake. "But not this time."

Mom said you had to take me. You can't go without me.

Nico. She faced me defiantly. *Get the fuck out of my way. Move. Now.*

Then it all happened so fast. "She went to go around me but I wouldn't move. I just stood there."

Move your fat ass!

"She went over to this side." I stepped to the side of the trail where it dropped off by the lake, not too close. The jutting rocks and steep side below us, with only one length of rusty metal handrail between two posts, unchanged from four years ago.

She had sighed loudly, trying to push her bike around me. But I wouldn't move. I stood, arms crossed. I had never stood up to her before. I had never defied her. I could tell she was confused, angry. This wasn't the Nico that she knew. What did I think was going to happen? That she would say, "Nico, you're totally right. Come with me. Come hang out with me and my boyfriend. You can watch us make out."

Suddenly, she dropped the bike to hit me and I ducked. I stepped back and felt my right foot slide beneath me, over the edge, just a few inches from the end of the handrail. I turned, suddenly scrambling, falling, as the ground seemed to move from under me, rocks and dirt scraping as I slid. I looked up, reached over for the metal post of the railing just as I heard the sound of something hitting metal. It took me a moment to realize that it was the back of my own head. I blinked and saw blackness, heard a rushing in my ears.

Then silence.

"Nico!" I heard Sarah scream. It sounded so far away.

I tried to sit up, realizing too late that my legs were hanging over the side of the trail, over the lake hundreds of feet below. My head had luckily caught the post of the railing and had broken my fall, leaving my upper body still on the trail, but barely. I scooted back, clinging to the railing, my head throbbing. Next to me, I could see Sarah's bike toppled, the wheel hanging over the edge. I felt the back of my head where the pain was the worst and found my hair was matted and wet. When I looked at my hand, my fingers were covered in blood. I gagged, crouching on my hands and knees. Now Sarah was going to be in trouble, real trouble. Mom and Dad couldn't ignore this.

When I tried to stand, everything went in slow motion, and my vision swirled with black spots.

I held the rail and turned to look for Sarah. I couldn't see her anywhere. She had left me, gone on to the picnic area to meet Max without me like I knew she would. I was alone. She had left me here, hurt and bleeding.

But she had also left her bike. That didn't make sense. Why did she leave her bike?

My head was hurting so badly, I could barely keep my eyes open. I heard, from below me, over the edge, a sound of tumbling pebbles and sand. I glanced over the side of the trail and saw something light gray dangling from an exposed root about halfway down. Her sweater. A gentle breeze caught it, and it drifted, softly landing in the water far below without a sound. I watched it fall, cashmere, floating, like a soft, gray dove.

Her bike was on its side, the wheel still spinning round and round, *tick-tick-tick*. I watched as her sweater slowly darkened with water and then sank beneath the surface.

SARAH

WHEN I GOT A chance, I looked up the missing girl, Sarah from Pennsylvania. It didn't take long to find all kinds of links about her, and the huge sum of money her family was offering for her return.

She did look like me, but prettier. Her hair was thick and blond where mine was a drab brown. Her eyes were a light hazel and mine had a muddied green-brown shade. Her skin was perfect and glowed, and I had the complexion of someone who ate a lot of fast food—and some days didn't really eat at all. The shape of our eyes was the same. And the nose. I was a little bit shorter than her and weighed about ten pounds less. But we could have been sisters, or maybe cousins. We were even the same age, give or take six months. I saw why the clerk at the store thought I could be her. Because I could.

Every now and then, when I had some time and nothing else to do, I would look her up online and see what was going on with her case. I wondered what it was like to be so loved, to have a family that missed you, wanted you back. I scanned through the photos of her beautiful, perfect parents, her sister. The news articles about her boyfriend, so handsome and worried, leaving the police station after questioning. Her best friend, with fingerprints on the bike, pinched face like a sour lemon. But after a while, there was nothing new to report. Just the same old pictures over and over, two years old, then three. It was starting to look like they were never going to find Sarah Morris, dead or alive. Until suddenly, they did.

CHAPTER 25

I HAD AN IMPULSE to try and get the sweater, but how? The sides of the cliff were too steep, rocky, dangerous. My sister was going to be so mad, this was my fault. She would make it my fault.

"What happened then?" Sarah asked. It was the first thing she had said to me since we started up the trail.

"I just stood there. Maybe it was only for a few seconds. It all happened so fast," I admitted. "My whole body was shaking, my head." I reached back, feeling for the tiny scar that only I knew was there. The words caught in my throat.

I waited for her. I thought she would come back around the corner of the trail. Say: *Nico, you giant baby, you should see your face right now! Come on, let's go. Don't tell Mom and Dad about this, or you know what you'll get.* She had played tricks on me before. I waited for her to jump out and scare me. But she didn't.

Maybe it wasn't that bad. Maybe she was okay. The *tick-tick-tick* sound of her bike tire slowing down pulled my eyes from the lake.

"Then what?"

I looked at Sarah, trying to read her face, but her sunglasses hid her eyes from me.

"I didn't know what to do, so I picked up her bike and I rode it down, fast. I was looking for someone, to get help. At first. But then . . ." I stopped. This part was so hard to explain.

When I came out of the darkness of the path and into the light of the park, it was filled with kids and happy families, picnicking and swinging and playing at the fountain. I suddenly realized that if I got someone to help, and we went to get Sarah, how it would look. What my parents would think. What could I say? What had happened? I didn't really know. I only knew that it looked bad, the way Sarah and I always fought. Maybe she did go on to meet Max without me. Maybe she was fine. I tried to tell myself that, but the image of her sweater, in the dark water . . .

It had all gone wrong. So wrong. Unless I was never there.

"I rode her bike all the way down to the gate and I locked it on the rack. I checked the handlebars, to make sure they weren't stained with my blood. Then I unlocked my bike and took off for home."

As soon as I got back, I stripped and threw my clothes into the washing machine. I rinsed my sneakers with the garden hose. The scrapes on my elbows were easily covered with a shirt. I showered and gently washed my hair, the water running red from a small cut that I could feel with my fingertips, just at the back. It formed a lump just beneath the surface that hurt for days, through all the days of the police asking questions, the first days of Sarah being missing. But it healed, after a while, like all wounds do.

"How did you go?" Sarah asked, pulling me from the memories. "How did you ride home? Did you take the same route we just did to get here?"

"Uh, yeah." I tried to remember. "I think so." I liked how she was being so calm, so exact. Not emotional. Not saying *How could you, Nico. What is wrong with you? Did you even look for her? Why didn't you call someone?*

"So anyone coming to the park that day could have seen you," she said, looking out over the lake. She held her hand up to shield the glare. "How deep is this lake?" Sarah asked.

"It's about thirty feet, some places deeper," I said, my voice breaking. "It's part of the park now, so there's no boats or fishing or anything allowed."

"Swimming?" Sarah looked at me and I could see my own face reflected in her sunglasses, a warped shadow image of myself.

I shook my head. "Part of it is in the Seneca reservation, so nobody is allowed."

"They never searched the lake for her?" Sarah asked.

"They never had a reason to—everyone thought she had disappeared from down in the park, by where her bike was," I told her.

She nodded. "Let's go." She took my hand, even though it was damp with sweat, and led me down the main trail. When the trail was wide enough to walk side by side, and the lake was no longer in view, she linked arms with me.

"What does Paula know?" she finally asked.

I shook my head. "She just said that she saw me."

Sarah glanced over at me. "Saw you where—on your bike? Or in the park?"

I knew what she was asking. Did she see what happened to Sarah. Did she see the fight, the fall.

"I don't know, all she said was that she saw me, she wrote it in an email."

"What else did she say?" Sarah asked.

That's not Sarah.

"Nothing," I told her.

When we reached the bottom of the trail, Sarah led me over to our bikes at the rack. "She probably saw you here," she said, standing by the rack and looking around. "Or riding back to the house."

I nodded. That made sense. I didn't want to think of what else she might have seen, maybe even more than I had. Did she see Sarah's body hit the water? Did she watch her die?

"Why didn't she just tell the cops then?" she asked.

"After Sarah went missing, Paula said she was home the whole time. She couldn't change her story; the cops already suspected her. I guess she just thought it would all go away. And it did, for a while."

I tried not to remember what it was like after Sarah first disappeared. The waiting, for someone to find out the truth. To be discovered. After two years, it felt like maybe there was hope. We were all going to be okay. But then, the reporter from the paper called, and all the terrible facts and speculations from that day reemerged. There was no escape from Sarah.

"There was this newspaper article, like two years ago. It made Paula look really bad, Max too. She started sending me emails after that. I just didn't know they were from her, until now," I said. "I guess she was hoping she could push me to confess, to admit something, to clear her name so that she wouldn't have to say anything."

I leaned over to unlock my bike and saw stars floating in front of my eyes when I stood up, blackness creeping in from the corners. Sarah grabbed my arm. "Nico?"

"I'm okay." I blinked, and the blackness pulled back, the stars disappeared.

She held my arm firmly, and leaned in. "This stays here, all of it. Let it go. You understand?" Her face wasn't mean, but serious. "This stays here," she said again. When I nodded, she let go of my arm.

She looked at me thoughtfully and I could tell that she wasn't worried about herself, about being found out as a fraud, as a fake. Sarah knew exactly what she was doing. She was worried about *me*. About how to protect me. "You need some lunch, and it'll buy us more time, come on," she finally said. "Are you okay to ride?" She motioned to my bike and I nodded. I could do it.

She climbed on Mom's bike and rode toward the gates. And just like that, I followed her, leaving the park, leaving the picnic trail and Crystal Lake behind me, as if it had never happened.

I followed Sarah through the streets to a café near the park, letting the breeze dry the tears on my cheeks.

SARAH

MA HAD DECIDED TO take in another foster. She had done this before and it never really worked out. I could remember two kids she tried to take in, but we always ended up giving them back when she got arrested for something or we had to leave one town and set up in another. Why child services would even let her take in a foster kid was beyond me, with her record, but they did—again and again.

"It's not going to be like when you were little, Libby," she said. "I was still using then, I was out of my mind. Not to mention that— well, I won't even call him a man, because a real man doesn't put his hands on a little girl. Monster, more like it."

That's how Candice came to live with us. Adorable, about seven, her hair a light brownish-red halo over her freckled face. This kid should have been starring in movies, but she was living with me and Ma in north Florida. She started working her magic right away, when Ma took her to Toys "R" Us with a hot card that almost got rejected. When Candy started to cry, the clerk took one look at her and let Ma out of there with a new dollhouse (that really was for Candy) and a game system worth about six hundred dollars (that was for resale). And they gave Candy a huge swirly lollipop, for free. I sat in the back of the car feeling useless, while Candy played with her new dolls and Ma laughed her ass off.

"You should have seen her charming them! We're ordering pizza tonight, Candy—anything you want on top," Ma said.

"Can we get soda too?" Candy asked in her sweet little girl voice.

"All the soda you can drink, sweetheart."

CHAPTER 26

SARAH QUICKLY TEXTED MOM as soon as we were seated at the café, letting her know that we went on a bike ride and were grabbing lunch. I had forgotten to bring my phone—we had raced out so quickly, I'd forgotten everything. My mind went to the black bag under Sarah's desk, and now I understood. She was ready. She had prepared for this months ago.

"Do you have your credit card?" I asked Sarah, looking over the prices on the menu.

She looked up from her phone. "Don't worry about it."

When the waiter came over, she smiled up at him. "Would you mind if we moved to that two-top in the corner? It's a little too sunny for us here—is that still your station?"

The waiter picked up our water glasses and moved us over to the other table. I had noticed that Sarah had this funny way of calling tables in restaurants by the number of seats—a "two-top" or, like when we went to the Italian restaurant with Mom and Dad, making a reservation for a four-top.

Once we were situated at the new table, tucked away from everyone else, Sarah ordered for both of us. I watched how quickly she reassembled her face into something different: bright, open, pretty, when the waiter came over. It was as if the morning had never happened, no one would know what this girl, ordering so calmly, had been talking about moments before. Just as he was about to turn away, he stopped and spun around. "You look familiar, both of you—have you been here before?"

Sarah looked down, blushing. "You might have seen me and my sister on the news, a while back—"

The waiter stopped her. "Get out! You're her? That girl who was"—he dropped his voice—"kidnapped?"

Sarah nodded. "I don't remember much about it, to be honest."

"And she doesn't like to talk about it," I interjected.

"Of course." The waiter nodded, his eyes still wide.

As soon as he walked away, Sarah leaned in. "We won't need a credit card now, you'll see." I glanced over at our waiter, behind the counter whispering to an older man wearing a name tag. I looked away fast and met Sarah's eyes across the table.

"Remember when you had to pick something for your science project, and you wanted to do it on organic food?" Sarah asked me.

I nodded, taking a sip of my soda.

"And what did I say?" Sarah asked.

"Um." I thought back. "You said that I should do something that we had actually studied that year, something on earth science."

"Right." Sarah studied the wrapper on her straw for a moment. "Because that's what your teacher expected, even though he never said it. He wanted to know that he had taught you something. And you gave him that."

"Yeah, my homemade seismometer," I said, laughing. I would have never come up with it on my own—entirely Sarah's idea.

"From the chapter on earthquakes that you had studied," Sarah pointed out. "And you won second prize—would have been first if not for that little twerp."

She was talking about Walter Curtis, the kid in my grade who had been bumped up from ninth because he was so brilliant. His project, on solar power, was amazing and had taken first. But really, he deserved it.

Sarah went on. "You gave Mr. Gardner what he wanted, what he expected—not what he asked for, but what he wanted, deep down. A pat on the back." She smiled. "'See what I learned, Mr. Gardner? You taught me this,'" she said in a high-pitched voice. "And you got an A and a red ribbon."

The waiter was back, hovering over us with the older man. "This is my manager, and he just wanted a word with you girls, if that's okay," he said, putting our sandwiches down in front of us.

"I was so pleased to hear the news that you were back, Ms. Morris, and I wanted to shake your hand and let you know that you are always welcome here." The older man looked flustered, shaking Sarah's delicate hand in his large, meaty paw. "And lunch is on me today, dessert too—anything you girls want."

"That's too kind." Sarah shook her head. "Really . . ."

"I insist. I'll have the waiter bring the dessert menu by as soon as you're ready, and again, it's just so good to know that you're home and safe. It really is." He stood in front of us, as if waiting for something.

"Well, I can't thank you enough. I'll be sure to let my parents know of your kindness, too," Sarah said softly.

The man nodded and smiled. "Enjoy your lunch," he said before walking away.

Sarah grinned and lifted a sandwich to her lips, taking a big bite. I still had no appetite, but picked up a fry and ate it slowly. Sarah had said to leave my confession at the park. *This stays here.* I watched her eat her sandwich as if nothing had happened, as if it were a regular day. She was able to do that, somehow. I had to do it too.

"I want you to remember Mr. Gardner when that detective comes back tonight, okay?" Sarah wiped her mouth with a napkin.

"Remember that you're going to give them what they want, whatever that is. Even if they don't know that they want it. Answers. The truth, even." Sarah glanced over at the manager and gave him a little wave. "Just enough truth. Give them what they want, and it's going to be okay."

SARAH

IT WASN'T LONG AFTER Candy came to stay that I decided my time with Ma was up. "We'll miss you, won't we, Candy girl?" Ma said, but she didn't beg me to stay or anything. I was over eighteen. I needed to be on my own anyhow.

I moved in with another waitress, Sheila, who knew that I cribbed credit card numbers at the restaurant but wasn't in that racket. She knew me as Melissa "Missy" Carter, and I never did tell her my real name. Melissa was some blond chick who had drunkenly dropped her ID at the last restaurant where I worked. I didn't take anything else from her—not her credit cards or cash—so she never reported her ID stolen. She probably just got it replaced, which meant I could be her at the same time, which worked for me. I had a record in Gainesville. Not easy to get a job, even waiting tables, when they can look up your real name and get a list of your arrests in about five seconds. But Melissa Carter had a clean record. She also had light blond hair. That's why I'd dyed my hair platinum—not my best decision, but Melissa Carter from Tampa was a bottle blonde, so I was too.

Things were going okay for a few weeks, even a month. Tips were good, and Sheila was pretty cool, but her stepfather wasn't. One too many times, he "accidentally" walked in on me in the shower and that was enough to send me packing. I grabbed my sleeping bag and my backpack and got on the bus that night, leaving Sheila a note and a few twenties for her troubles.

I rode all the way to the beach, just wanting to feel the sand beneath my feet again. But when we rolled into West Palm, it was raining buckets. I hid under an awning at the bus station for hours, eating bags of chips and soda from the machine until it let up around dusk. It wasn't the best time to walk the tourist traps, looking for a waitressing gig, so I decided to hit the beach and wait until the next morning. A dry bench and my sleeping bag would do just fine—with my hood pulled up, you could barely tell I was female. Or so I thought.

That first night, there was a group of guys, maybe from a frat at the local university, who decided it would be fun to harass some homeless folks on their way out of the bar. They mistook me for an old lady or something. It didn't go well, especially when they realized that, while I was a lady, I wasn't exactly old. "Hey, blondie!"

one of them yelled after me as I made a dash. "Come on, we aren't going to hurt you." They were so drunk and stupid, I lost them quick, but I left my sleeping bag and backpack behind, hiding in an alley where the smell of wet garbage, rotting in the humidity, made me gag up the Doritos I'd eaten for dinner. When I returned to the bench at dawn, my stuff was completely gone—of course.

I tried to clean up in the public beach bathroom, but my hair hung dirty in knots. I finally managed to rake my fingers through it and twist it into a ponytail. Still, I looked shabby, and had no clothes to change into for my job hunt. I went into a few of the tourist joints, looking for waitressing gigs. No one was hiring—either they didn't like my looks or they really didn't have any openings.

Finally, one place gave me a paper application and I sat down to fill it out with a borrowed pen. I still had Melissa Carter's license, so I used all of her info, except for the social security number, which I just made up. When they got around to figuring out that it was wrong, I'd have a new one for them.

When I was done, the manager, a large round woman with a hint of a dark mustache over her lip, told me to sit tight for a minute and she'd interview me after the lunch rush. The guy behind the counter handed me a paper container of salty fries and I took it with thanks and about ten packs of ketchup. After I inhaled the free snack, I looked up to see the mustached lady and the guy behind the counter sort of whispering and staring over at me. I wiped my face with a napkin and scuttled to the bathroom, thinking that I must look pretty terrible. But on my way to the ladies', I saw through the big windows at the side of the place as a cop car pulled up not too discreetly right outside. I turned around to see mustache lady, her eyes as big as burger buns, watching while the cops came to the door. I guess ole "Missy" finally managed to report her license stolen—and everything I'd been up to in her name for the past couple of weeks had caught up with me.

I didn't wait around to find out. I ran into the bathroom and locked the door, sliding out the tiny window over the toilet before the cops could get back outside and around the building. I booked it down an alley and into an open screen door that led into the kitchen of another neighboring restaurant. But that was the end of my life as Melissa Carter. And I couldn't be Liberty Helms anymore. I wasn't really sure who to be, or what I was going to do.

When the sun went down, I used the last twenty dollars I had in my jeans. I bought a cup of coffee and two doughnuts and a cheap touristy sweatshirt with a hood in a size extra large that would have to double as a blanket. I curled back into the same bench at the same bus stop when it got dark, with no idea of what to do the next day. Going back to Ma's wasn't really an option. Besides, I didn't have the scratch for a bus ticket. Maybe I could call Sheila and see if she might come down to pick me up. I thought about Ms. Lay, my old math teacher. Even if there was a way to find her, I doubted she would remember me. Her most promising student, now sleeping, nameless, at a bus stop.

They woke me up with a flashlight in the face, and I didn't lie when I answered that I didn't know who I was or where I was—that was the truth. For a moment anyway. Then it all clicked into place. Was I Liberty? Or was I Missy? No. I had no name. I had nowhere to stay. No one cared about me, or ever really had. I had about fifteen cents left in my pocket. I was no one now.

"How old are you?" the lady cop asked. "You look like a minor. You a runaway?"

"My name is . . . my name is Sarah," I said, before I even knew what I was doing. The image of the girl's happy family swam before my eyes. Her blond family, the huge reward, the handsome boyfriend. A family that loved her. People who missed her. Who wanted her back. "And I have a sister named Nico."

CHAPTER 27

BY THE TIME WE got back to the house, it was late afternoon. As we rode our bikes down the streets, the sun cut through the leaves and trees in a flashing mosaic on the sidewalk. Somehow the heat had broken, the cool breeze lifting our hair.

I felt drugged, as if someone had slipped something into my soda. But really all Sarah had done was listen. She hadn't asked why— why I didn't call for help. Why I didn't tell the truth. Why I put the bike in the rack and rode home like it had never happened. Maybe she didn't ask because she knew that I didn't have the answers. Instead, she had listened to my truth and she hadn't questioned me. She still loved me, she was still on my side. Just like a real sister.

I watched her ride in front of me, on Mom's bike, her blond hair blowing in the breeze. I tried not to think about what her life had been like before she came to us. Where she had been all those years, the things that had happened to her. Why she wanted, needed a family so badly. She was with us now, and I wanted her to stay.

When we pulled our bikes into the driveway, Mom came out and stood on the front steps, a deep line between her eyebrows. "Detective Donally left a message—he said he came by earlier."

Sarah smiled, coming up the stairs. "Oh yeah, almost forgot, he came by just as we were going out. He didn't say why though, right, Nico?" She turned to me, her face open and warm, as if she had nothing to hide.

"I thought he was just checking in," I said, going around Mom and into the house.

"Let's jump in the pool," Sarah suggested. "It's still hot out."

Mom came in behind us, closing the door. "He's coming by tonight, after dinner."

"Who, the detective?" Sarah asked. She opened the fridge and took out an orange juice. "Nico, you want?" she asked, shaking the bottle.

I shook my head. "I'm going to go put on my suit." I went upstairs and sat on my bed for a minute, taking deep breaths. So he was coming back, just like Sarah said he would. But it would be okay. Just like Sarah said. I mechanically tied on my bikini and went into the bathroom, looking at my face in the mirror. Our hike had put color into my cheeks, my hair was blown by the wind of the bike ride into a summer-tousled look that suited me.

I looked good. My eyes weren't red.

I noticed now, for the first time, that I'd gotten my hair cut at the exact length that Sarah's had been when she went missing. I leaned in and blinked. "Hi, Detective, what can I help you with?" I whispered to the mirror. I bowed my head, just slightly, the way Sarah always used to do when she wanted to charm someone. "Oh, really, you're too kind." I repeated Sarah's words at the restaurant to see how they felt on my tongue. I smiled at my reflection. Sarah was right, I could do it.

We swam, Sarah in the shallow end while I practiced my dive. I did a jackknife off the edge of the pool and let myself drift aimlessly down, until my toes touched the rough plaster at the bottom. I floated there, eyes closed, feeling my hair swirl weightless around my face, until I couldn't hold my breath any longer. Is this what it was like for her? Then I pushed my feet against the bottom and rose to the top, gasping for air when I surfaced, the sun on my face.

"You okay over there?" Sarah asked, running her hands through the water on either side of her raft. She didn't like to go in the deep end and I suspected it was because she didn't know how to swim. There would be time for that, later in the summer. I could teach her.

We lay in the afternoon sun, side by side, as if it were a normal summer day. I rolled over and looked at Sarah, her eyes closed, her thin body stretched out next to mine on the lounge. "Sarah, when

Gram was here, and she wanted to talk to you on the porch that night—what did she say?"

"Huh?" Sarah shielded her eyes and looked over at me. "What made you think of that?"

I shrugged. "I just remember when you came in, you'd been crying."

Sarah closed her eyes again and tilted her face up to the setting sun. "Gram said, 'If it's not really you, please never tell me.'" Sarah paused, as if thinking for a moment. "She said she wanted to die knowing that her granddaughter was okay, that she was home and safe."

I swallowed hard and rolled over onto my stomach. We stayed together, quiet, until the sun dropped below the trees and it started to get chilly. By then, Mom had dinner on the table and Dad was on his way home. We sat down, taking our usual chairs—I now sat where Sarah always had, and she sat across from me. Before Mom served the pasta, I hadn't been hungry at all, but somehow I found myself devouring every bite and taking seconds before Dad even had a chance to sit with us.

"Where did you girls go today? You're both eating like wild animals!" Mom laughed.

"We just rode around, it was a great day for it," Sarah answered. "You don't mind that I borrowed your bike?"

"Of course not. Actually, that's something we should bring up with the detective tonight. You know, we never did get your bike back, it was 'evidence' or something."

"I bet it could use a tune-up, too," Dad chimed in, taking the salad bowl from Sarah. "I can tinker with it this weekend if they can get it back to us."

Sarah caught my eye across the table, as if checking to be sure I was okay. I smiled at her and she quickly changed the subject: "We had lunch today at the best café—the manager was so crazy nice," she started, telling the story of how they comped our lunch, and the amazing carrot cake we shared for dessert.

As soon as Sarah and I started on the dishes, the doorbell rang and we knew exactly who it would be. I dried my hands slowly and closed the door to the dishwasher before turning to see Sarah, waiting for me in the doorway. Her gaze was calm and steady as she silently put an arm around my shoulders.

"Nothing, not even a cup of coffee?" Mom was saying as we walked into the living room. Detective Donally had come alone this time, so maybe it wasn't as big a deal as we thought.

He took a seat opposite the couch and laid a large folder on the coffee table. "No, thank you," he said, his mouth forming a grim line. He watched closely as Sarah and I sat together on the couch.

"So there's been some news on Sarah's case, I gather," Dad said, hiking up his pant leg and crossing one leg over the other.

The detective took a deep breath. "Not exactly, just a new development." He looked over at me and then opened the folder, pulling out one sheet of paper from the top. "You all know a Paula Abbot, is that correct?"

At the sound of her name, I felt my body tighten. I had been right.

"Yes, she's a friend of Sarah's," Mom said quickly.

I laid a decorative pillow across my lap and traced its swirly maze pattern with my finger.

"She contacted us last week with some information, something she now says she forgot to tell us during the initial interviews, after Sarah's disappearance," the detective went on.

I saw Dad tilt his head to one side, suddenly interested.

"Paula says that she saw someone on that day, at the bike rack, near where Sarah's bike was locked," Detective Donally said.

"Wait a minute—I thought Paula hadn't seen Sarah for days—they were fighting, wasn't that the story?" Dad interjected.

"Yes, what was she doing at the park?" Mom asked. "Wasn't her alibi all along that she was at home?"

Detective Donally nodded. "She says that after she called Sarah that morning—the call that we have logged on both of their cell phones—she decided to go to the park to meet Sarah and talk more."

I watched Dad's face as he squinted skeptically, a look he took on when he thought someone was feeding him a lie. "Oh really?"

"That's what Paula claims currently," the detective went on. "And she saw someone there, acting suspicious."

"Who was it?" Mom leaned in and asked. "Someone we know?"

"It was Nico," Detective Donally said. He waited a beat, as if pausing for a reaction from us. I continued to trace the pattern on the pillow without looking up.

"So?" Sarah said, looking from Mom to Dad for a reaction. "Nico goes to the park all the time. We were just there today on our bikes, right, Nico?"

I nodded and glanced up for a moment.

"I agree, I don't see quite where this is going," Dad said. "Does this help the investigation at all?"

"Well, Nico told us she was home all afternoon on that day, so there is a discrepancy in her statement," the detective pointed out.

Dad let out a laugh. "There is a *discrepancy* with Paula's statement. First she's not at the park, now she is. And four years later she decides to share this information? This is nonsense."

"Paula is wrong. Nico wasn't at the park that day. Isn't that right, Nico?" Mom's eyes were unreadable, the same way they had been when I asked her about Sarah, about the differences that I knew she had noticed. She didn't blink under the watchful eye of the detective.

I just nodded, not trusting myself to speak.

Dad added, "And Sarah is back now. Why does it matter where Nico was that day, or what she did?" He was so calm and collected. The news from the detective was not a surprise to him, either.

"That's the other thing. Paula seems to believe that—well—" He paused, looking at Mom carefully. "She thinks this isn't actually Sarah." Before Mom and Dad could even react, he went on, "Paula says that the girl we all think is Sarah is actually an imposter, a stranger who has assumed her identity."

"That is ridiculous!" Mom laughed. "And I think we all know where this is coming from." She looked over at Sarah. "Tell the detective about Max and Paula, why she might say these terrible things about you and your sister."

Sarah quickly explained the relationship between the three of them, how Paula had been dating her boyfriend when she returned home and how awkward things had been between them. How Paula blamed Sarah for Max breaking up with her. She went on to add that Paula had been cold to her since coming home for the summer—the two former best friends had seen each other only a few times. "I definitely got the idea she was not happy with me," Sarah added. "I mean, I can hardly believe it, after everything that's happened, but she still seems mad at me for stuff from years ago."

The detective nodded. "While I understand that, Paula gave us a list of discrepancies—between the Sarah that she knew and Sarah now. It's everything from her fingernails to her height and stature. I have to tell you, the list has raised some questions." He held out a piece of paper to Mom, but she shook her head, refusing to touch it.

"I think we can all agree that Sarah has changed, and honestly I think a lot of this is very hurtful to her, to be compared to her old self—my God! Look at what my daughter has been through." Mom looked over at Sarah as if to check that she was okay. "How can we stop Paula from saying these awful things?" Mom asked.

"Well"—the detective took in a breath—"we don't usually run a DNA test if the family confirms a missing person's identity, and they are, uh"—he stumbled here—"still living. But we could." He looked over at Sarah. "We would need your approval, of course. Then we could put these questions to rest."

Mom sat stone-faced for a moment, and Dad didn't move. But Sarah suddenly spoke up: "Sure, I'll take a test," she said, shrugging as if it was no big deal.

"Now wait a minute, Sarah has to give DNA to prove who she is? She's Sarah! I mean, just look at her! This is getting crazy." Dad leaned forward in his chair.

The detective glanced over at him. "It will take only a few minutes, the test is painless, a swab in the mouth."

"Fine, when? Tomorrow?" Mom said in clipped tones.

"I could take her down to the station now, have her back to you in an hour at the most." Detective Donally stood and looked over at Sarah again.

"Whatever is easiest," Sarah said calmly, without looking at me.

"No," I heard myself say.

Every head in the room turned to look at me.

"I have something to tell you." My voice didn't even sound like my own.

"Nico, don't," Sarah said quietly. "You don't have to."

But she had no idea what I was about to confess.

SARAH

SOMETIMES, WHEN I'D BE sitting on the couch, Candy would just come up and put her arms around my neck, call me "sissy"—short for sister. She would hang on me and play with my hair, saying, "You're so pretty, Libby." I knew it wasn't real, that Ma was teaching her, just like she taught me, how to use what you've got to get what you want. If you're pretty, use that face. If you're curvy, use that body. If all you have is charm, then smile and let 'em have it.

Candy would usually follow up with a request: Do you have any gum? or Can I watch TV now? Can I stay up late with you and Ma? It was never a hug just because. It was never love.

When I woke up in the children's shelter that morning, and the Morris family came into the room, it was like a whole different feeling. Love, everywhere. I felt it, when Mom wrapped her arms around me, in the tears on Dad's face. Love, unconditional.

Family love, the real kind. It felt so good, I wanted to jump up and yell. I wanted everyone to know that I, Liberty Helms, had a family, finally, a real family of my own, people who loved me. But they didn't love me, they loved Sarah, the missing girl. Or did they?

Nico stood in the doorway that day, stiff but obviously so fragile—she was as broken as I was. I knew it would take some work to win her over. Kill 'em with kindness, Ma always said. But it wasn't so easy. It became clear pretty fast that Sarah and Nico had not been super-close sisters. Then I realized it was more—how she flinched when I sat next to her. She was scared to even come into my room. Sarah had hurt her, physically and emotionally. She hated Sarah, or she had.

She wasn't the only one. I saw it in Paula's eyes, challenging me. The way Mom and Dad reacted to the most simple kindness, like it was a gift, a revelation. Sarah had not been a nice person. She was more than a bitch, she was downright terrible. And it was my job to clean up her mess if I wanted this family to be mine.

Max was a lost cause: he wanted the cold blond beauty he had worked so hard to win over, the most popular girl at school, and I wasn't her. So, after breaking Paula's heart, he moved on. Paula's friendship with Sarah had been based on competition, and if I wasn't playing, what was the point? So I started with Nico and worked my way up. Funny thing was, once I got to know Nico, I really did like her. It wasn't pretend. Sweet, damaged kid. Why had Sarah tortured her? I'd never know now, because Sarah was dead. And Nico—innocent Nico—had watched her die.

CHAPTER 28

"SARAH HAS A TATTOO," I blurted out fast. "She did it herself, right before she went missing."

"What?" Mom said, her mouth hanging open, eyes wide.

Sarah looked over at me. I was probably the only one who noticed her tiny smile, the squint to her eyes. "Nico, how could you tell everyone? You promised," she said.

"Sorry, Sarah," I said quickly, watching as Detective Donally paged through his folder.

"I remember something . . ." he murmured, looking for a sheet of paper. "Your boyfriend also knew about this," he said. "Max?"

"Ex-boyfriend, but, yes, of course he knew, it's his initials," Sarah said, looking down and blushing a bit.

"Oh my goodness," I heard Mom say quietly.

Detective Donally pulled a sheet of paper from the folder, saying: "Max did tell us about the small tattoo when we were originally investigating the case. He offered it up as evidence of their affection for each other. I believe, it says here"—he turned the sheet of paper over and read—"not only do you have a tattoo, but he has a matching one, of your initials, on the right hip?"

Sarah stood and pulled down the side of her shorts, showing at the hip, right where her bone curved beneath the skin, the tiny letters in black: an interlocked *M* and *V.*

Mom glanced at Sarah's skin and let out a sigh. I couldn't tell if she was thrilled or horrified. "What on earth were you thinking?" she said to Sarah. She shook her head, then turned to the detective. "And if this was in your records of the investigation from years ago, why is it the first we're hearing about it?"

"I'm sorry," the detective started to say. "I didn't see the point in sharing anything hurtful about your missing daughter. Max made it clear that it was a secret they had. . . . Honestly, I kept it in the file in the hopes that we could use it for, well"—he paused for a moment—"for body identification."

Dad put his hands out in front of him. "This was a long time ago, she was only fifteen. I'm sure Sarah would never do something like that now."

The detective stood and gathered his file together quickly. "I guess a trip down to the station isn't really necessary. I'll just add a note to her file that a visual confirmation of Sarah's identity was made." I saw now that he was blushing slightly—either embarrassed at having challenged Sarah's authenticity or the intimate nature of the tattoo, I couldn't tell which.

Mom stood up, her chest blotchy and red like it got sometimes when she was mad. "And what about Paula? What are you going to do about her? I have half a mind to press charges against her!"

"Don't worry about her—we'll get in touch and let her know that Sarah's identity has been confirmed. Really, Mrs. Morris, I do think she means well," Detective Donally said, backing toward the door. "She seems to be a troubled young woman."

"You can tell her if she wants to cause any more distractions from the actual investigation into Sarah's disappearance, I will come after her, with a lawyer," Mom added, marching him out. She undid the lock and swung the door open hard.

"Sorry to have interrupted your evening, and we'll be in touch if there's anything new—actually new—on Sarah's case," he mumbled as he scooted down the walk and out to his car.

As soon as the door closed behind him, Mom turned around, her face tight with anger. I waited for her to turn on me, grab me by my shoulders, shake me until I told her everything. But instead, she launched into Paula. "Honestly, what is wrong with that girl?" Mom said fiercely. "I'm about to call her mother. And you . . . a tattoo." She turned to Sarah, shaking her head.

"All I can say is that I wish I'd never done it—if I could take it back I would." Sarah had tears in her eyes.

"You *are* going to take it back, we're having it removed as soon as possible, I'll make an appointment with the dermatologist," Mom declared.

I could tell from Sarah's face that she was on the verge of bursting out laughing, but instead she pulled Mom into her for a hug. "I made a lot of mistakes back then," she said quietly.

Dad's eyes got that teary look and I could hear Mom sigh. "You were just fifteen." She pushed a lock of Sarah's hair behind her ear. "And you're not like that anymore, are you?" A look passed between them that I tried to read, but it was fleeting.

"Let's focus on what's important here," Dad said, like he was running a meeting at work. "Our family is back together, and nobody—not Paula, Detective Donally, Detective Spencer, Max, or even a silly tattoo—is going to change that, not ever."

Spontaneously, the family that never used to hug formed a tight circle, our arms around each other. We stood in the foyer, our heads bowed. It felt good to be complete again.

SARAH

EVEN THOUGH SHE COULD have, Nico never asked. Maybe she didn't want to know how I broke my arm. How I got the burns. Why I had a couple of teeth missing. Maybe not knowing made it easier to believe the lie between us.

I know it did for me.

Because I never had to talk about it, slowly the memories faded of Liberty's life. And Sarah's memories became mine. But the visits to the psychiatrists weren't totally useless: one of the docs gave me a prescription that really helped me sleep and was perfect for those nights when I got my period and the cramps were killer. Knocked me out flat. The other doctor had some techniques that also helped with my bad dreams: no caffeine before bed, no stimulants of any kind. I spent a half hour in bed every night reading, usually a romance or something light—fashion mags. The nightmares still came, but less often, and then they seemed to stop altogether.

When I caught myself thinking about those days, the darkest ones with Ma, I just changed my thoughts, like changing the channel on a TV—another bit of helpful advice from the doc. I see myself hiding under that porch, the one attached to the trailer, with the dust filtering down between the boards, while Ma wrestles with the cops just over my head, saying she lives alone—she has no children. And I switch to another thought—me and Nico, out at the pool. Shopping at the mall. The way Mom looks at me when I come home from work, like seeing me come through the door is the best part of her day. She says that I make her proud, and I hear the words of my math teacher, all those years ago: I'm profoundly proud of you. I can banish those dark memories because now I am loved. I'm done running, pretending to be someone else. I'm Sarah Morris now. I am Sarah.

And I know I am loved.

EPILOGUE

I KNEW MY SISTER was dead. I felt it in my body, as if my bones could tell me the truth. They were, after all, her bones too. The same parents had created us, the same genes, the DNA, the stuff that makes us who we are. We were made of the same, she and I, and so no one knew her better than I did.

And I was there when she died.

We go back to the park every year on her birthday, my sister and I. We never actually set foot inside, just stand outside at the gates. March 11, early spring, and almost always raining or damp. A dozen white roses, wrapped in a yellow ribbon, left on the brick wall at the entrance arch.

And every year, on that day, there's a huge celebration with our family—bigger each year, it seems, with Mom and Dad, Grammie and Uncle Phil and our cousins. We are still making up for lost time, for the four years when there were no birthday parties. Sarah invites her friends, new friends—there's no one from her past in her life anymore. Where Max and Paula have disappeared to, I really don't know. I heard Paula was in graduate school out West. Max was doing his residency somewhere in New York City. I'd lost touch with both of them, as had Sarah.

When Sarah first came back, I let myself believe: What if it is her? What if she crawled from that lake, from the deep, with no memory of who she was, and someone took her in? She was back, with no idea what had happened, no knowledge except for her name. That would mean that I was not guilty. That I hadn't kept the secret for four years. That she was still alive. And she looked like her, so much. Everyone thought it was her. My parents embraced her, everyone did.

I wanted to believe, especially because she was so changed. She was the sister I always wanted. And I was that for her. I wanted to forget. But I never would. The secret would live with me forever, and it was Sarah's secret now too; there was no escaping the truth.

But on the edge of our happy, restitched lives there was always, for me, a dark anxiety. I worried that Paula would snap again some-day, and persuade another detective, a cop, of what she had seen, what she thought she knew, and implicate Sarah and me in the pro-cess. I was haunted by the possibility that someone might discover the real Sarah, whatever was left of her. What if they drained that lake, or dragged it? What if there was a terrible drought at some point, and her bones emerged from the silt?

Every now and then, a reporter gets in touch—when some other kid goes missing, especially if it's in our state—or some kid is returned. They want interviews or photos, but we always politely decline, referring them to the Center for Missing Children for information on Sarah's case, without giving any personal details. I understand now why Mom never wanted Sarah's return publicized: She didn't want to face the scrutiny, the doubt, the questions. Better not to know, not to ask. I was starting to see just how wise my mother was, a trait I had never respected or recognized in her, now I not only admired, I emulated.

On my last trip home from college, Tessa came over for dinner with the family, and I let Sarah try her experimental highlighter on my hair—something she had mixed up in the lab at beauty school. It smelled like rotten eggs and burned my forehead a little bit. "When I get done with the chemistry side, I'll add a fragrance, promise," she said. She stepped back with the plastic gloves on her hands to admire her handiwork for a moment while Tessa made faces behind her.

After she rinsed it off, I had a few sections of lighter blond hair in the front, but the strands were also brittle and frayed. "Too much peroxide," Sarah murmured to herself, jotting something down in a notebook. "I'll put a deep conditioner on tonight, that'll be better by morning. But look, it worked—natural blond made blonder, right?"

"I think it looks pretty good—summer in a bottle," Tessa said, putting her hands on my shoulders and looking at me in the mirror.

"I think you just came up with the product name: Summer in a Bottle. Mind if I use that?" Sarah was serious.

I looked at my hair in the mirror over the sink, startled by the almost-white highlights around my face. It wasn't really my look, but I knew Sarah could fix it tomorrow, dye it back a more honey blond. Or maybe I'd just leave it, tell my friends at Princeton, proudly, that my sister was creating a line of hair products and I was her guinea pig, supporting her every effort—her partner in crime.

A team.

After all, what are sisters for?

ACKNOWLEDGMENTS

This novel was inspired by the mysterious true crime case of Nicholas Barclay, a Texas boy who disappeared in 1994 at the age of thirteen, and the young man who impersonated him and insinuated himself into the Barclay family three years later.

I am grateful to all my early readers, especially my agent, Brenda Bowen, and her assistant, Wendi Gu. Special thanks to Nanci Katz Ellis, who read the manuscript more times than I did. To the Ross men, Damon and August, I owe more thanks than I can ever express; you both have taught me the true meaning of family and love.

A deep bow of gratitude to Donna Bray for her unwavering support, and the editorial team of Balzer + Bray for their talent, hard work, and dedication.